BURGUNDY AND BODIES

WINE VALLEY MYSTERY BOOK 1

SANDRA WOFFINGTON

Red Summit
Publishers

ISBN-13: 978-1-944650-28-5 (ebook)

ISBN-13: 978-1-944650-29-2 (paperback)

BOOKS IN THE WINE VALLEY MYSTERY SERIES

Prequels:
Merlot and Murder: The Beginning (FREE)
Beaunoir and Blood: For Joy (FREE)
Grand Cru and Gangs: Steele's Story (Dead Silent Boxed Set)

The Series:
Burgundy and Bodies, Book 1 (May 2019)
Pinot Noir and Poison, Book 2 (May 2019)
Syrah and Swingers, Book 3 (May 2019)
Rose and Rocks, Book 4 (June 2019)
Grenache and Graves, Book 5 (Aug. 2019)
Shiraz and Slaughter, Book 6 (Sept. 2019)
Pinot Grigio and Pesticide, Book 7 (Nov. 2019)
Gamay Noir and Ghouls, Book 8 (Feb. 2020)
Claret and Carnage, Book 9 (May 2020)
Viognier and Venom, Book 10 (July 2020)
Frascati and Fratricide, Book 11
Fume Blanc and Fire, Book 12

Wine Valley Mystery Books 1-4 Boxed Set
Wine Valley Mystery Books 5-8 Boxed Set

More murder, mystery, and mayhem to come . . .

OTHER BOOKS BY THE AUTHOR

WARRIORS & WATCHERS SAGA SERIES

EPIC MYTHOLOGICAL FANTASY

Seven ancient gates of evil will open, unless a quirky group of teens become warriors.

"Original and consistently entertaining from cover to cover." **Midwest Book Review**

Evil Speaks (Reader's Favorite 5-Star Review)

Evil Hears (coming soon)

Evil Sees

Evil Touches

Evil Feeds

Evil Deeds

Evil Desires

———

STAND ALONE HISTORICAL ROMANCE

Unveiling

What would you sacrifice to fulfill your destiny?

STAY UP TO DATE

In appreciation of each and every reader, I created a Facebook group called *Woffington's Reading Warriors: Mystery, Murder, Magic & More* specifically for readers to join together and share their interests, discuss books, and to communicate directly with me and fellow Reading Warriors.

I post updates, previews, new releases, insider information, and awesome offers in this group.

Visit my website at sandrawoffington.com.

Follow me on Amazon, Facebook or Instagram.

Come for the Mystery—Stay for the Magic!

ACKNOWLEDGMENTS

If you love this series, it is because of my fan ARC Readers and the pros on my team.
Thanks for your energy, your belief in me, and your support!

ARC READING WARRIORS
Lisa Oster
Donna Hopson
Julie Bawden-Davis
Dara Davis
Jo-Anne Jackson

PROS

Editor: Beth
Cover Artist: Judy
Marketer: Jynafer

To future authors—
Go for it—write the story!
It will haunt you until you do.
And when it's done, the characters for the next book show up and
start the process all over again.

1

Anne Martin strolled along the moonlit path that snaked beside Goldrush Creek, an offshoot of a river that ran southwest from Riverside, passed through Wine Valley, and eventually spilled into the vast Pacific Ocean.

As Anne strolled farther away from Eugene's house and toward her own, she inhaled the earthy scent, a perfume of wild pleasure from the alders and oaks and sycamores. The chaparral and sagebrush and tall scrub grass brushed against her arms or ankles as she squeezed by narrow points in the path, but she welcomed their touch. She enjoyed living beside the creek.

Life had finally taken a turn for the better.

She'd made nothing but mistakes for the past decade. But today had brought a new opportunity, and maybe her last chance to get it right.

A twig snapped behind her.

Anne spun around. "Is anyone there?" She listened intently but heard only the gentle babbling eddies of water swirling at the shoreline or insects chirping or the water lapping as it rushed down river.

Anne walked on. She laughed, remembering how she had flirted so openly at the poker table. All in good fun. The men loved her playfulness, all but Kenneth. Maybe she was free of his hold on her at last.

Another twig snapped. Closer.

Anne's eyes darted from one moving shadow to the next. Her heart raced inside her chest. Her breathing quickened.

She froze as a figure approached. "What are you doing here? Did you follow me? Leave!"

A fist flew through the air and connected with her jaw. The impact shot pain through her head and neck and stunned her senses. She twisted and fell into the dirt. Her cell phone flew from her hand. She remained motionless, breathing hard, and attempted to regain her senses.

Anne pushed herself up until on her knees. She reached for her sore jaw and took a deep breath. She'd just begun to get her bearings when a jagged rock flew at her blond curls and smashed against her skull.

The force whipped her body around. She plummeted to the ground. Her back slammed into the dirt, knocking the air from her lungs. Searing pain surged through her head and neck. She tried to blink away the dizziness.

Anne moaned as she reached up and touched her head. Her fingertips felt moisture and jagged flesh. She pulled her hand away. In the moonlight, she saw dark liquid—blood.

Arms dove under Anne's armpits and tightened around her torso. Someone dragged her. A shoe slipped from her foot.

In a single movement, the dark figure spun her onto her stomach.

Splash!

Anne landed face down, half in and half out of Goldrush Creek at a shallow spot on the shoreline. She knew the spot well. She sometimes picnicked here alone in the shade of a nearby oak tree or waded in the shallow water with bare feet.

The water refreshed her. She lifted her head and sucked in air.

A hand pressed against the back ofAnne's head. Her face plunged into gooey mud. Her arms flailed uselessly, like a beautiful white swan with broken wings.

In a final flap and flutter, her arms fell to her sides. Her life spilled into the creek and washed downstream.

2

D r. Kenneth Grant awoke in his red, convertible Porsche Boxster, parked outside Anne's single-story yellow cottage.

Kenneth moaned and fought to get his bearings. The sun filtered through the branches of an old oak tree, shooting shards of glassy light into his bloodshot eyes and, it seemed, into his skull. Memories of the night's events seeped into his brain, like blood from a wound.

Kenneth licked his dry tongue over even drier lips. He glanced at the passenger seat. Anger and self-loathing raged within him. He grabbed the nearly empty vodka bottle and hurled it into the air, letting out a howl like a wounded animal. The bottle smashed against the trunk of the oak, shattered, and rained glass and vodka onto the tree's old roots.

Kenneth opened the car door and set his feet on the ground. He almost wished he'd spared the vodka and drank it to ease the pounding in his head, the raw pain in his stomach, and the ache in his muscles.

He dragged his feet as he approached Anne's house. He

knocked on the door, rubbed his cheeks to get the blood flowing, and leaned against the doorframe.

"I'm sorry about last night! You know how I get, Anne. You have to admit, you pushed my buttons."

The truth is, he barely remembered last night after he left the poker game at Eugene's house. He stopped by a liquor store, picked up a bottle, and guzzled it in the parking lot. Once the clear liquid washed away his common sense, he drove back to Anne's house to win her back. He passed out.

Had he even stepped from his car? He glanced down at the cuffs of his pants and picked away a burr. As he did so, he clenched and unclenched his hand. It ached.

He yanked his cell phone out of his pocket and called Anne's number. He felt flushed. He needed water.

Kenneth turned his head. He heard a faint ring in the distance. He set one foot before the other, marching off toward the path beside Goldrush Creek.

Kenneth redialed Anne's number each time the phone switched over to voice mail. The rings became louder. His heart raced faster with each ring. He quickened his steps. The sounds of the rippling water taunted him, heightening his need to slake his thirst.

For a split second, his mind erupted in rage as the possibility crossed his mind that he'd find Anne with Eugene. But reason intervened: he could never hear Anne's phone ring from Eugene's house. It was too far away.

Kenneth squeezed past a stretch of trees where the path narrowed. A tree trunk caught the sleeve of his blue cotton shirt, and ripped it, as if to stop him from going farther.

"Anne!" he shouted.

It was close, the ringing. Like he'd find her around the next bend. Wild grasses pricked at his ankles, stabbing him through his socks. "Anne!"

Another ring. Clear. Finite.

Kenneth turned the corner.

Anne's body lay face down. Her legs sprawled out on the bank. Her chest and head rested in the shallow water.

Kenneth raced to her side. An agonizing moan left his lips as he set his fingers gently against her cold throat.

No pulse. Pallor mortis had left her skin deathly white, almost translucent.

Kenneth stroked her soft, blond curls, as he'd done so many times before. His face contorted. He threw a fist up to his mouth. He struggled to remember the night before.

He wanted to drag Anne out of the water to safety. Instead, he flung himself backward, until he sat on the bank. He observed her body, hoping to ignite a memory. He'd seen plenty of dead bodies in med school and after, but not Anne's. Not pretty Anne's.

Panic set in. Could he have done this? No, not to Anne. He fought the urge to vomit.

He thought of running back to his car and getting the hell out of there, but he'd smashed the bottle against the tree. He knew enough about forensics to know he could be traced to Eugene's house and to Anne's. Cameras might have recorded his having bought the bottle. Running only made him look guilty. Was he?

Kenneth's hands shook violently as he pressed 9-1-1. When the dispatcher answered, he could only utter, "She's dead. Anne's dead."

Detective Max Pride King arrived first. Blonde, blue-eyed, twenty-six, and well-built, he would pass for a surfer, if not for his navy-blue tactical pants and polo shirt with the gold Wine Valley Police Department logo. In the week or so that Max had taken off to mourn his father's death and arrange for the funeral, it seemed like his entire world had turned upside down. He understood why his father had complained, "I hate change."

The police station had moved from its humble beginnings on Stagecoach Street to the new civic center plaza and City Hall a block up and on a hill. The architects had given it the façade of an upscale Spanish adobe mission, including clock and bell tower.

Max also had a new boss, Captain Jayda Banks, his former lieutenant and partner. That part he liked immensely, although Jayda's first words as captain were, "Max, if you think I nagged you before—that ain't nothin' compared to how I'll come up your grill if you slip up under my command. You hear me? No monkey business." Her tone was softer than her word choice, but Max knew she meant it.

Jayda took her career seriously, a career his father, former Chief of Police David King, had nurtured, and she would not let anyone, even his son, jeopardize her command. Max gave her an "Understood, Captain. I won't let you down," which he thoroughly meant.

Max had only recently made detective. The celebration at the station was one of his last memories with his father, before David stuck his nose into a case that they closed together. But the drama resulted in a heart attack, a ride in an ambulance, and David King's funeral. His father would not have it any other way—going out with guns blazing.

Max never wished for a new dead body to arrive on his doorstep, but he desperately needed to get back to work to pull his head out of the pit of grief that had consumed him. This case gave him that opportunity.

Max found a man sitting in his car before the victim's house. He opened his notebook. "Are you Dr. Kenneth Grant?"

"Yes."

"I'm Detective Max King." As Max drew closer, he smelled fresh booze and saw the broken bottle at the base of the tree. "Bad night?"

Dr. Grant sighed. "After I left the poker game, I grabbed a bottle, drank a bit, and came back to see Anne. I must have fallen asleep in my car."

"Fell asleep or passed out?" asked Max.

Dr. Grant stepped out of his car and glared at Max. "Up until last night, I hadn't had a drink in over a decade. This morning when I woke up, I hurled the bottle at the tree. Happy now?"

Max jotted a mental note of the man's restrained anger and wondered if he faced an alcoholic or a killer—or both. He'd let the evidence speak for itself. "Where's the body?"

"This way." Grant explained as he walked forward, "I called Anne's cell phone. It rang. I followed it and found her."

Max followed Grant. "Did you touch anything?"

"Only her neck to check for a pulse." As Kenneth made the last turn, he glanced over his shoulder and added, "I didn't kill her. I'm sure you think I did. But I loved her."

As soon as Max saw the body, he pointed to a pair of white alders. "Wait there."

The ME had already been notified and would arrive soon. Max combed the ground, careful not to disturb evidence as he approached the body. He knelt down and felt for a pulse, even though he had no doubt about the conclusion. His gut burned with a single desire—to find justice for the girl who's life had spilled into the brackish water. "You said you called her cell phone this morning, and it led you here. Where is it?"

Kenneth rang Anne's number.

Max followed the sound. He located the phone along the path where dirt met scrub brush. He put on sterile gloves and moved some long grass aside. He dropped the phone into an evidence bag. He spotted something else. He bagged it too, a silver cigar clipper. As he turned, he spotted a flat black shoe.

Max observed Anne's lifeless body. She wore the matching shoe, like a macabre Cinderella. Max noticed scuff marks in the dirt. She'd been dragged.

A chill raised the hair on Max's arms. This was no accident.

I n no time, the site crawled with a CSI team dispatched by the county Bureau of Forensic Services and the medical examiner. The woodsy scene swarmed with people wearing white, hooded suits and blue gloves. Some technicians established a perimeter. Others set up a search grid. Others snapped pictures or collected evidence.

While the team worked, Max interviewed Dr. Grant, who looked like death. After obtaining the basics of name and contact information and the rudimentary details of discovery, Max asked, "When did you last see Anne Martin alive?"

"I just saw her last night. We played poker at Eugene's house. He lives farther down the path."

"Who else was there?"

"Eugene, his daughter Cynthia, and Shane Drake, a local pharmacist. Deon Walker, a friend of Anne's from the hospital —but Deon left early. I'd never met him before. Lee Chen also came, but he left early too. And Chief Goldsby was there."

Max stopped writing the moment he heard the name of the current chief of police. Frank Goldsby had replaced David King after David's first massive heart attack three years earlier, which led to bypass surgery and early retirement. The more recent heart attack took David's life. Goldsby had it in for Max—his newest detective. Max's father had become legend—he roamed around town like a small-town sheriff, no matter how large Vinoville grew. People loved him. That set a chip on Goldsby's shoulder when it came to Max.

Max snapped out of it. He had a job to do. He set his pen against his notebook. "Did Anne Martin have any enemies, anyone who would want to hurt her?"

The doctor cringed. His face contorted. He paced in a small circle. "No. Anne was a kind woman. She was my Marilyn Monroe, you know. I mean her personality. Anne is...was...she was so beautiful but fragile."

"Fragile how?"

The doctor pursed his lips.

Max had seen it before—no one wanted to rat out a friend, even if he or she was dead, and even if it meant solving a crime. "She's dead, Dr. Grant, and the only chance I have of finding who did this, if there is foul play, is if you tell me as much as you can about her."

"Anne was a compulsive gambler. She owed money to the casino." Kenneth folded his arms over his chest.

"How much?"

Dr. Grant rubbed his face as if to wake himself up from a bad dream, but he could not wipe away his bloodshot eyes or the bags beneath them. He had a smoker's face—hollow eyes and lips tinged yellow. His cheeks bristled with a days' growth of beard. "Can I smoke?"

"No. You'll have to wait," said Max. "How much did she owe the casino?"

Grant grew frustrated, "She stopped talking to me about it. I'd given her loans before, and she always paid me back, but last December, when she asked me to help her out again, I cut her off. I thought it would help. I thought she'd get help. I came back last night to tell her that I'd give her the loan."

Max assured him, "Casinos don't usually murder their clients, especially those making payments. But I'll check it out." Max wondered if Anne had taken a loan from someone less friendly, but even if true, she'd be roughed up, not murdered. The dead don't pay up.

"Max!" called Angelo.

Max closed his notepad and stuffed it in his pocket. "Dr. Grant, you can go for now, but stop by the station and give us a formal statement."

Grant assured he would, and Max strolled over to the ME.

Angelo, a stocky man, fiftyish, with silver-gray hair and a close-shaved beard, gave Max a preliminary report. "Blunt force trauma, most likely that rock sitting near her head."

Max informed him, "Her shoe and phone landed over there."

"She has mud in her nostrils, which suggests someone pushed her face down. I won't know more until I get her back to the shop."

"Thanks, Angelo." Max had gotten used to Angelo referring to the Bureau of Forensic Services lab as "the shop." Angelo had come by it honestly. His father, an Italian immigrant, had opened an auto repair shop that specialized in foreign cars. Angelo worked there until he began his residency as a forensic pathologist. In a way, Max figured that Angelo probably saw each body as a broken car, one he hoped to diagnose—not to repair but to answer difficult questions: "How did it break and when?" It was Max's job to determine, "Who broke it."

Max eyed the landscape. His brain assembled the clues and reconstructed the crime. Anne's cell phone had landed near the path, which meant it had to either fly out of her hand—or that was where the blunt force trauma occurred—and she was dragged to the water—during which time, her shoe fell off.

Someone pushed her head down into the soft silt and held it there. If she fell and hit her head, her shoe and phone would have been near her body.

As Angelo coordinated the removal of the corpse, Max headed back to Anne's house.

Despite his grim reason for being near the creek, Max admired this tiny stretch of his backyard that he'd never seen before. The creek surged beside him; the sun caught the canopy of the trees, and a rabbit scurried under a bush, its heart racing like Anne's must have raced when she was attacked.

4

Max entered Anne's cottage, stepped past a CSI tech, and into a rustic living room with a southwestern rug in blues, golds, browns and reds. A log-like pine daybed served as a couch. Gray wolves traversed the snowy brown and white comforter and pillows. Indian knickknacks sat on shelves and side tables, giving the room a country air. A basket of wood sat next to a black wood-burning stove.

Every detail informed Max that Anne had an affinity for the gray predator that traveled in family packs. Did she want a family? Or did she need the strength of a pack?

Max entered the master bedroom, careful not to get in the way of a second technician, who opened drawers and searched through them.

Colorful Talavera painted pots and vases overwhelmed Max's eyes with a dizzy display of color, tempered only by a white goose down comforter and pillows embroidered in large vibrant flowers. It was like stepping into a flower market in Mexico.

The bed had not been slept in. Anne never made it home.

Anne liked color. Lots of it. Why? Did she need to grab

attention, excitement, thrills? Was her life so drab that she needed to spice it up? Did it remind her of home, a place from her youth? Did the colors simply make her happy?

With gloved hands, Max opened a nightstand. He pushed aside over-the-counter sleeping pills, overdue bill notifications, sample medications in single-dose packages, birth control pills, casino chips, and two photos.

Max picked up the pictures and gazed at Anne about ten or fifteen years younger. A long-haired boy with a mustache had his arm around her. They clung to each other like lovers. Another picture displayed an old man standing in front of a manufactured home. Anne's father, maybe. He and Anne had similar features, but Anne smiled and he scowled. Anne was even younger in this picture. A teenager.

The overdue bills from five to six months back told him that Anne had financial problems. A newer bill showed her up-to-date. Either she hadn't stuffed more overdue notices in the drawer or she had solved her problem. *What did you do, Anne? Did you dig too deep a hole to climb out of? Did you ask the wrong people for a ladder and they sucked you down?*

In the master bathroom, Max found more Mexican pottery. But the bright colors could do nothing to bring life back to the yellowed vinyl floor and chipped tub.

Anne kept the place neat and clean. She was organized, even meticulous. Maybe driven to perfection. Or had she organized her house but failed to organize her life?

From the master bedroom, Max opened the sliding glass door and stepped out onto a concrete patio with a white plastic table and four chairs. The view of the creek and the never-ending landscape created a vast wild space, the complete opposite of Anne's little house.

Max sat on a chair. Where did Anne take a wrong turn? It was hard to imagine that way out here in this desolate but beautiful spot, Anne could have just been in the wrong place at the wrong time. In all likelihood, she knew her attacker.

And that person savagely slammed a rock into her head and held her underwater—but who? And why?

Max followed the path once again, passing by the crime scene, and made his way to the house where Anne had played poker.

Pristine, white, wooden fences cordoned off considerable property. It was a perfect setting for horses, but there were none. The large, custom-built, single-story home sprawled along the creek, like a country manor.

Max knocked on the front door, on which hung a floral wreath with a wooden placard that read "Home Sweet Home."

Cynthia Carter swung open the door. Her chocolate-brown eyes shot from Max's face to the gold Wine Valley PD insignia on his polo shirt. "Can I help you?"

Cynthia had a round face and pale-skin devoid of make-up, which gave her a dowdy appearance. She pushed her thin brown hair, parted in the middle, behind her ears. She had to be mid-thirties, but her floral cotton dress and a white cotton apron, which read "My Secret Ingredient—Love," made her more of a life-sized fifties-era doll than an adult.

Max flashed his credentials. "Detective Max King. I'm afraid I have some bad news. Can I come in?"

Cynthia opened the door wider. "Of course, Detective King." She yelled down a hallway off of the foyer. "Papa! There's a police detective here!" She turned back to Max. "You know what? I'll go get him. He was up late last night playing poker with your chief. Make yourself comfortable."

Max crossed a grand A-framed room with bare-beamed construction. Large windows acted like a living painting of the creek at the far end of the room. A massive stone fireplace to the right took up one wall. To the left sat a kitchen with granite counters and white cabinets. A dining nook with a round table sat before French doors, leading to a back patio. The living room bloomed with florals—floral couches, drapes, and burgeoning vases of faux bouquets, which created a garden that could never exist in the hot, dry weather outside.

Beside the fireplace, a large Victorian doll house sat upon a built-in white cabinet and gave the room a homey touch, like a child lived here, but Max imagined it belonged to the girl who'd answered the door. It was, no doubt, a childhood prize worth keeping.

Compared to Max's comfortably disheveled, refurbished hacienda, this room had a feminine touch—everything in its place. The scent of freshly baked bread filled his nostrils. His stomach grumbled.

Cynthia bounded into the kitchen, while Eugene lumbered across the room, still dazed with sleep. Eugene wore slippers and a hunter green bathrobe emblazoned with his monogram in gold lettering. It gave his bald, slim face and skinny, tall frame a hint of sophistication—forced, not natural—like an actor playing the part of a country squire.

Cynthia slid a spatula under scones cooling on a baking sheet and set them on a wire rack. "Detective King? Can I make you some coffee or tea?"

"Nothing, thanks," said Max.

Eugene settled on the sofa, while Max settled himself in an oversized floral armchair.

Before Max could begin, Cynthia swept beside him and set down a floral, porcelain plate, on which sat a hot and fluffy blueberry scone and a glass of water. "Fresh from the oven. You men never eat right. I insist."

Cynthia handed her father another plate before dashing back to the kitchen and bringing her father a cup of tea. She dashed once more, bringing back a plate and a cup of tea for herself.

Max waited until the girl sat down. He needed the pair's

undivided attention. Max whipped out his notebook and pen. "This is never easy. Anne Martin is dead."

Eugene had just set his cup to his lips, but it fell from his hands and broke the saucer in his lap in two. Hot liquid spread over his thighs and the floor. It splashed on the sofa and coffee table.

Eugene jumped to his feet, as did Cynthia, who set her cup down, rushed to fetch a towel, and proceeded to wipe down her father's robe, the coffee table, and the sofa. "Oh, Father. What a mess you've made!"

"Never mind that, Cynthia. She's dead? Did you hear? How?" asked Eugene, collapsing into the sofa.

Cynthia kept wiping the carpet and sofa. "Well, staining the sofa isn't going to help, Papa. I'll get you another cup."

Max thought Cynthia's reaction an odd one, but he'd seen so many variations over the years: there were the yellers, the fist-pounders, the wailers, the dumbfounded, the zombies, and the fainters.

Cynthia obviously needed to stay busy and organized to restore order. She set a new cup of tea before her father. "I don't mean to appear callous. What happened, Detective King?"

Max watched the pair for their reactions. "We don't know yet, but she was found beside the creek this morning. Dr. Grant had stopped by to see her. He found her. We don't think her death was accidental."

Cynthia blurted, "Oh, that's dreadful! Dr. Grant dated her. He smokes, and he didn't always speak kindly to Anne, or to you, father."

Eugene protested, "Anne broke up with him months ago. That's old news. And he's a doctor. Not a killer. Anne, was she...assaulted?"

"We don't have any information yet," said Max. "What can you tell me about her. Did she date anyone after Grant?"

Eugene sipped his tea and lowered his head as if in contemplation.

Cynthia didn't hesitate. She let out a huff. "I liked Anne, don't get me wrong, but she used her charms. She was on a roll last night. You know what I mean, detective. Tossing her head, making uncouth jokes, batting her eyes to get attention."

"Cynthia!" reprimanded Eugene. "Have respect."

Cynthia insisted, "It's the truth, Papa. He needs to know the truth. Isn't that right, detective?"

"Yes, it is," said Max. "The more you can tell me, the better the chance of finding out what happened. Did Anne leave with anyone last night?"

Eugene shook his head. "No. She left when the chief won the last hand, around midnight, I guess. That's when everyone left."

Cynthia sipped her tea. "It was about a quarter past. Deon —that's Deon Walker—and Lee Chen—Mr. Chen owns a flower shop in town—they left earlier, but Shane, Anne, Kenneth, and the chief left together. Dad went to bed, and I finished cleaning up. I can't stand waking up to a mess."

"When did you go to bed?" asked Max.

"Oh, maybe a half hour later, at most," said Cynthia. "I'd been putting away the food and tidying up while the game came to an end. I don't play cards. There wasn't much left to do. The crystal wine glasses needed to be washed by hand. And I put some food away."

"Can you think of anyone who would want to hurt Anne?" asked Max.

"Not a soul," said Eugene. "She's a nurse at the hospital. She takes care of people." His eyes fell to his lap. "I was fond of her. We all were."

Cynthia let slip a sigh of contempt.

Eugene stammered, "Anne...she was so full of life. She made us all laugh."

"Did you ever date Anne?" asked Max.

Eugene blurted, "Me, no. Never dated."

Cynthia added, "After mother passed, father dated Mayleen, Lee's daughter. But she broke his heart and ran off."

Eugene sighed, "One of these days, you'll leave me too, won't you girl? Go off and marry Shane."

"Shane Drake?" asked Max, checking his notes.

Cynthia blushed and nodded. "That's right."

"What do you do, Eugene?"

"I own a mortuary and funeral parlor, one of the oldest in town. It belonged to my father, Crane Carter, but he passed. I've expanded business over the years. Cynthia helps out. She'll take over the family business one day."

"Did you notice anything unusual about Anne's demeanor last night? Was she upset at all? Anxious?" asked Max.

Eugene swallowed a bite of scone and washed it down with a sip of tea. "She'd been anxious since she and Grant broke up, but not last month and not last night. She seemed like her old self, laughing, truly happy. Last night, she won a few hands, but she kept playing until she lost it all to the chief."

Cynthia agreed. "She did seem happy. She asked if I needed help cleaning up, but it was late, and I knew she was tired, so I said 'no.'"

Max set a card on the coffee table. "If you think of anything, no matter how small, call me. And stay in the area. I'll need to speak with you again, I'm sure."

Eugene nodded. "Of course. We have no travel plans."

Cynthia jumped to her feet, wrapped Max's untouched scone in a paper napkin, and walked him to the door. She handed Max the package. "Take your scone. I won't take no for an answer."

Max took a bite to be polite. He preferred donuts, crumble or glazed, but the light, warm sweetness hit his tongue and instantly satisfied his stomach. "This is good. Thank you."

Max munched on the scone as he walked back along the creek to Anne's house. He passed by the scene of the crime— now as pristine as before. Anne no longer lay next to the creek. He could imagine her walking home along the serene path awash in moonlight, unaware it would be her last stroll beside the flowing waters and earth-scented bank.

Max's father had taught him to get to know the victim— Who was Anne? How did she think? With whom did she associate? Did she have secrets? Only by knowing the victim, by seeing Anne walk along the path in the moonlight, could Max piece together the last moments of her life. He imagined her rising up from the bank of the river and continuing her walk home beside him. He could see her toss her head and implore, "You will find out who killed me. Won't you, Max-y?"

5

Max wasted no time in making his rounds to the witnesses. Despite the fact that people routinely boasted, "I have nothing to hide," the truth was that almost everyone had something to hide. If they didn't worry about incriminating themselves, they worried about incriminating friends or family members. Occasionally, as with Eugene and Cynthia, they blathered openly, bickered even, dropping plenty of clues. Cynthia objected to Anne's flirtatious ways; Eugene welcomed them.

Max knocked on the door of Shane Drake's house, a beige and cream suburban tract home with a dead lawn and scraggly shrubs that desperately needed water, but city water rationing had left his neighbors' lawns the same shade of brown. The few green lawns meant the occupants paid the exorbitant water bill for excess summer usage.

Max had to ring a few times before Drake swung the door open.

The moment he saw Max's Glock on his hip holster, Shane smoothed down his unkempt curly red hair and swiped at his beard. He didn't seem to care about the wrinkles in his pajama pants that bore blue and white San Diego Padres logos, but he tugged at the black T-shirt that stretched tight over his big belly.

"Shane Drake, I'm Detective Max King. I'm afraid I have some bad news. Can I come in?"

Shane curled a finger, the sign for "permission granted," and walked away. Drake smelled of beer. He held his back and stretched as he led the way to the small living room, a man cave. Darkened windows indicated Shane probably worked night shifts.

Shane settled into a massage chair, flipped the control, and let out a sighing moan as rollers ran up and down his spine.

Max could not help but notice the kitchen was a mess. A clump of soiled kitchen towels sat on the white-tiled counter; food wrappers and processed food boxes over-filled a tall plastic trashcan; a pair of pans on the stove contained dirty water, like they had been left to soak but still needed cleaning.

Max somewhat appreciated the fact that he wasn't the only disheveled human being on the planet. But he made a mental note to pick up when he got home, so it would never get this bad.

"Bad back?" asked Max.

"Beyond bad. I worked construction in college. Had a nasty fall. Been in pain ever since. Good thing I'm a pharmacist—not that I self-medicate—that was a joke. Only legal prescriptions, which I can't take as often as I'd like, because I work as a pharmacist. It's complicated."

"I wasn't implying anything," said Max.

"Just saving us both some time. Something wrong at the pharmacy? Robbery?"

Max watched for Drake's reaction. "I'm sorry to inform you, but this morning, we found Anne Martin dead by Goldrush Creek."

Drake's eyes widened, his hands shot up to his mouth, his

jaw unhinged. He closed his eyes for a moment. "Good God, no. What happened?"

Max could only ask questions. "We're still not sure, but you can help. When did you see her last?"

"Last night at Eugene's poker game. We rotate. Eugene hosted."

"I already interviewed Eugene and his daughter, Cynthia. When did you leave?"

"Oh, I don't know. Midnight, half-past maybe. Chief Goldsby, Anne, Grant, and me. We all left together. Anne set off on the path home, and the rest of us hopped in our cars. Grant offered to walk Anne home, but she turned him down." As if struck by a sudden thought, Shane added, "Damn, if he'd have walked her home...maybe she'd still be..." He let the sentence die out and hung his head.

"Can you think of anyone who would want to hurt her?" asked Max.

"Anne? No," said Eugene. "She's a nice gal. Wait? Are you saying she was murdered?"

Max pulled back. "We don't know what happened yet. I hear she gambles?"

"Yeah, well, we all do—hence the monthly poker game—but all in good fun. Sometimes though, Anne, well, she doesn't —or didn't—know when to quit. Like last night. She was up twice but kept playing until she lost. But she makes good money at the hospital. We each bring a few hundred. It's nothing she can't afford, I think."

Max noted that Drake didn't know about her larger debts, which also meant that Grant hadn't shared the details of Anne's problem and neither had Anne. That seemed worth pondering later.

"I'm sorry to ask. This is routine. But did you have a relationship with Anne?"

Shane shook his head and let out a quick "Ha," followed by,

"No way. We were just friends. I'm not her type. She likes guys with expensive cars, like Dr. Grant."

"I heard they broke up."

Shane waved a hand in the air. "Yeah, well they do that a lot."

"Cynthia doesn't hold back with her feelings for Anne."

"Cynthia is old school, a real homebody. She's a doll. And a great cook!"

"You're dating her?"

"You could say that. Eugene invites me over a lot for dinner or to hang out, maybe watch television. He's been playing matchmaker. A man gets tired of living alone. I've asked Cynthia to marry me. She's thinking about it."

"Did Anne gamble at the casino?"

Shane shrugged. "I didn't hang out with her outside of poker nights."

"Anything unusual happen last night? I hear Anne was pretty flirtatious."

Shane laughed. "That's Anne. She's harmless. But, yeah, she fired it up last night. It riled Grant to no end. I think that was her point."

"Anything else seem out of the ordinary?"

"Deon was new. Friend of Anne's from the hospital. Nice enough. Left early, same time as Lee."

Max closed his notebook. "That's all I need for now. If you think of anything else, call me. Don't get up. I'll see myself out."

"I couldn't get up if I wanted to. Not until the pain meds kick in."

En route to the casino, Max began to see a bigger picture. Anne did have a secret—she gambled and she flirted. Was either one, or both, enough to get her killed?

Max's phone rang. "King."

"Angelo here. Can you swing by?"

"On my way."

Max strolled into the coroner's forensic facility and found Angelo in an autopsy suite.

Max could never get used to the smells—butcher shop meets hospital. The pungent air assaulted his nostrils immediately. He had witnessed his first autopsy during police academy training. A policeman had to understand how the medical examiner processed a body to learn how to better preserve evidence in the field and avoid contamination. But no matter how many times he'd visited this place, the windowless suites filled with stainless steel tables and jars of formalin creeped him out. Florescent lights hummed overhead, like drones of death, alighting displays of bone-cutting saws and dissection tools, vials with colored stoppers, scales, polished steel sinks, and a body freezer.

Max asked, "Find something interesting?"

With gloved hands, Angelo peeled back the blue drape, revealing Anne Martin's head and shoulders. A rock lay beside Anne's left ear. Angelo showed Max how the rock matched the impression made on Anne's skull. "This was not enough to kill her. She had mud in her nostrils and creek water in her lungs. She drowned. Another thing, look here." Angelo pointed to Anne's jaw.

"Bruising."

"Someone clocked her," said Angelo.

"Murder. Why?" It was rhetorical. Max wasn't really asking Angelo.

"My job only entails COD and TOD. Yours is finding 'who' and 'why.' One other thing. She'd had sex. Consensual, not forced."

"DNA?"

"Unlike the TV shows that give us a bad reputation—that

could take a few days. I'll try to rush it, but maybe you could nose around instead," said Angelo.

"There were only a few boys at the party. I'll start there." Max gave Anne one final gander. Her pretty blonde curls surrounded her head like a halo—but lake dirt tarnished the gold. She was no angel, but she didn't deserve to lie here on a steel slab with mud up her nostrils.

"Time of death between midnight and four A.M."

"Thanks, Angelo." As Angelo turned away, Max peered at Anne's face: her petite nose, full lips, and cherub-like cheeks. "I'll figure out which snake in the grass bit you. I promise."

6

The Golden Earth Casino sat at the southerly end of Wine Valley. Spanish invaders and the diseases brought by Europeans had decimated the ancestors of the local Native American tribe. But modern-day tribe members established the casino on reservation lands after California passed several acts that allowed Indian tribes to proffer legal gaming.

Over the decades, the tribe thrived. The casino grew to include a spa, a golf course, a hotel, and, through land purchases, the tribe expanded its territory as well. Gambling income paid for better schools and opportunities for higher education. The tribe also spread the wealth to neighboring towns like Vinoville by employing hundreds or through charitable donations to local projects like revitalizing the old western part of town that the locals called Grape Gulch or helping to fund the new civic center.

Max's father had a long-standing friendship with the tribal elders and casino executives. He'd worked to promote gaming laws, saying, "It's about time we righted a long-ass wrong."

Max had called ahead. A pair of beefy security guards in

tailored suits and wearing earpieces met him at the resort entrance, the fastest way to reach the business tower.

The security detail led Max through a maze of noisy machines with flashing neon lights that sounded like raining money: *ka-ching, ka-ching*. The carpet, a kaleidoscope of color, left him dizzy. It's browns, blues, and salmon shades rippled and criss-crossed, creating a psychedelic desert stream. Cold air chilled Max's cheeks.

No matter how often Max stepped into the casino, it felt like Las Vegas not Wine Valley. Max's friends had brought him here —a local rite of passage—on his twenty-first birthday, hoping the momentous date coincided with a gift from Lady Luck, and when it hadn't, they moved on to the sports bar and ended the night at Sal's Saloon in Grape Gulch to line-dance.

At the top of the elevators, the landscape changed to a place for business. Along the salmon-colored corridor, glass cases held shards of pottery and woven baskets and blankets and other tribal artifacts. But as soon as they veered left, away from the banks of elevators, the room opened up.

Busy employees sat in low-walled cubicles. Beyond them, floor-to-ceiling windows beheld golden rolling hills. Phones rang. Voices bumped into one another. Laughter or a sneeze punctuated the more mundane sounds, like the copier machine.

Max's escorts approached a secretary, who glanced up and said, "Go right in, Detective King. Can I get you a coffee or water perhaps?"

"No, thank you," said Max.

The first guard opened the door to the President's office, and the pair sandwiched Max between them, one in front and one behind. The guards waited by the door and let Max pass into the inner sanctum.

Max approached a massive mahogany desk, which was dwarfed by the large space, full of curio cabinets with artifacts and the same floor-to-ceiling windows that made the land the showpiece and backdrop of the room. The CEO seemed to be sitting in the hills, a modern chief conducting business like his ancestors before him.

Paul Lopez, a broad-shouldered man in an expensive gray suit, rose to his feet to greet Max. He had a tawny face, short-clipped gray hair, a square jaw, and piercing brown eyes. Given the mission history in California, Max was not surprised by Mr. Lopez's surname. "Paul Lopez. Please have a seat."

"Detective Max King." Max shook his hand and sat down in a plush leather chair. For this interview, Max had tossed on a navy blue jacket that he kept in his trunk. He felt awkwardly overdressed compared to his standard attire, yet underdressed compared to the man behind the desk.

"I pulled the file you inquired about, a Miss Anne Martin. May I ask what this is about?"

"She was found dead this morning."

Paul Lopez sighed. "I'm sorry to hear that."

"I've been told Ms. Martin owed money to the casino."

Paul opened the file. "She still owes us a little over fifteen thousand dollars."

"Whew!" said Max. "That's a big amount on her salary. How did that happen?"

Paul Lopez closed the folder and interlocked his fingers forming a line of defense. "As you probably know, we determine credit lines based on assets, but we pay particular attention to average balances in checking accounts. A couple of years ago, Miss Martin inherited from a deceased parent." Paul paused. His face fell, as did his voice. Both carried a tone of empathy. "I know we're in the gambling business, Detective King, but we're no different than companies that produce alcohol—none of us want our clients to abuse our products or services. Through this casino, we have been able to take care of our people and our neighboring community." Paul peeked at the file. "There was some trouble at the end of last year."

"What kind of trouble?" asked Max.

"Reviewing the file jogged my memory. Dr. Kenneth Grant came to see us. He spoke to the credit department. He made such a ruckus, I came down and spoke to him personally. It seemed like a better tactic than having security drag him out or calling the police to have him arrested. Dr. Grant cared for his friend. I could see that. I felt bad for Ms. Martin. Dr. Grant begged us to cut off her credit before she lost all of her inheritance, but I explained that I couldn't do that. Ms. Martin had rights too. She could sue us. I had my secretary give Dr. Grant information on gambling addiction facilities. That's all I could do."

"How much did she go through?"

Paul Lopez leaned back in his chair and let out a heavy sigh. "One hundred twenty-five thousand."

"You must have cut her off, though, as she had been asking friends for loans?"

"I don't know about any loans. We're not the only game in town, but I can tell you that she missed a payment about nine months ago. First time. She must have been out of money. We immediately froze her credit. She worked out a payment plan, but it would take some time for us to get the money back. If you're implying that someone at the casino..."

"No, Mr. Lopez. I assure you, these questions are part of a routine investigation. When was she here last?" asked Max.

Again, Lopez looked inside the folder. "Her player card shows minimal activity since we froze her credit. Looks like she still stopped in on occasion and played cash. A few hundred. Nothing big. She was in last week. She'd been making her payments. We keep tabs on our credit lines through routine credit checks. Missing a payment was the first sign of trouble.

You know, sometimes, reaching a low point is the spark that helps a person turn his or her life around."

Max stood up to leave. "Unless that person runs out of time to do that, like Anne Martin."

Paul Lopez rose to his feet. "I'm sorry I couldn't be of more help."

"Not at all," said Max, shaking Paul Lopez's hand. "Every bit of information helps piece the puzzle together." Max handed him a card. "If you think of anything else, give me a call."

"You sound just like your dad, except without the gosh-dern-its. I was at the funeral. I'm sorry he's gone. David King was a good man. A friend to the tribe."

"Thank you, Mr. Lopez. I appreciate that."

"Paul, please."

The guards, who hung at the back of the room, escorted Max as far as the elevators.

Max picked up to-go lunches and knocked on the door to Captain Banks' new office.

Captain Jayda Banks was a no-nonsense black woman with short-cropped hair. Although slender, she had a muscular build and an iron will.

"Come in."

Captain Banks had wasted no time in organizing her new space. A picture of her with her four-year-old daughter and her Marine husband in his beige camouflage utility uniform sat proudly on her desk. Her framed degree and commendations gave the room authority. Two large potted plants, one in each corner, added a spark of life. Framed photos of her officers showed her pride for the men and women under her command.

Max set a brown bag with a green Crisp and Crunch logo

on the desk. "I owed you this, and it seems like since your promotion, you don't get out to lunch anymore." Max checked his watch. It was two o'clock. His eating routine had taken a hit as well.

"Thanks, Max. I was just about to call for a delivery. Learn anything surprising so far about Ms. Martin?"

"Anne gambled away her inheritance, and she owed money to the casino."

Captain Banks said, "The casino doesn't kill off its customers. Debt with interest is in their favor."

"Anne was paying it off too," said Max, "until she missed a payment some months back and the casino froze her credit and put her on a payment plan."

"Good work. Keep it up. I see you got yourself a Crisp and Crunch bag too. You didn't go healthy on me, did you?"

Max held up his bag. "Baked potato, loaded with bacon and butter."

Captain Banks shook her head. "When you eat that, I want you to imagine a bullet coming at you right between the eyes— 'cause that's deadly, you hear me?"

"Death by butter—now that's an interesting investigation."

7

Max strolled through the entrance of the Wine Valley Hospital, barely a decade old, and through the honey-beige lobby with wooden tables and cream-colored high-backed chairs that would fit better in a nice hotel than in a hospital.

The public address system echoed an announcement about a sale in the gift shop. Max understood the concept of making a hospital seem like home—but it never worked, not really. Not with the smells of hydrogen peroxide, sweat, and illness, the latter of which smelled eerily similar to the decomposing flesh of a dead body. To offset the negative, cheery framed prints of colorful wildflowers adorned the walls.

Max rode the elevator up to the medical-surgical floor and checked in at the nurses' station, which had pastel green walls. Max left his jacket in the car. This made his Glock, which hung from a hip holster attached to his heavy duty belt, visible, but it was too hot for the jacket. Max caught the eye of more than one young nurse. He attributed the glances and smiles to his cop attire, but his polo shirt and tactical pants hugged his muscular body, and his blond hair, blue eyes, and white mischievous smile didn't hurt.

An Asian woman—short, slightly pudgy around the middle, and wearing hospital-issue blue scrubs—turned toward him. "Can I help you?"

"I'm Detective Max King. I'm looking for Deon Walker. I have a few questions in regards to a case of ours."

"Anne Martin?"

"Yes."

"We heard. We're devastated. I'm Lisa Nguyen, Deon's and, formerly, Anne's supervisor. Let me find Deon for you." She headed down the hallway, as if knowing exactly where to find him.

In moments, she returned with a black man, who had a muscular frame that Max guessed had been built lifting weights at the gym, not lifting patients. "I'll cover you, Deon. This detective has some questions for you. Why don't you go to the waiting area?"

Deon led Max to an open area with tall windows and plush beige chairs. A woman sat reading a book. Magazines of various types rested on cubic side tables.

Deon located a couple of seats in the corner, away from the woman. "I heard the news this morning. We're all in shock. I still can't believe Anne's dead."

Max asked, "You were at the game last night?"

"First time. Anne invited me before, but I always declined. I play some video poker at the casino now and again. I guess I thought it would be cool to play with the chief of police, you know. But I lost my three-hundred dollars in a couple of hours and left. Great food though! Eugene's daughter made us sandwiches and chili and bread—all real fresh. Plus strawberry pie. Still, wasn't worth three bills. Know what I mean?"

"How long have you worked at the hospital?" asked Max.

"'I moved here from Long Beach right after nursing school.

The hospital was fairly new and needed nurses. Rents are cheaper here too. And I do like the wineries, I have to admit."

Max asked, "Do you know any of Anne's family or other friends?"

"I didn't hang out with her after work, but I think her father died a couple of years back. Might have lived out in Hemet or Lake Elsinore. I don't know any of Anne's friends other than the ones I met last night. Seemed like an okay group. She's a good nurse, though. She really cared for her patients. I've learned a lot from her."

"Did she gamble regularly?"

"I think with the group, yeah. Like I said, I don't know her personal life much."

Max asked, "Was she anxious or upset last night?"

Deon lowered his voice. "Something was going on with her. But I don't know what. She seemed nervous all the time starting back some months ago. Distracted. But recently, she seemed like her old self. Last night, she had everyone laughing up a storm, everyone but Grant, her ex. It was playful, though. You know. I'd never seen that side of Anne before. She is—or was—a funny lady."

"What about Grant?"

"He's pretty intense. He just played his cards. Took a few smoke breaks. When Lee and I left, Grant and Anne were arguing outside. They stopped when they saw us."

"Did you hear any of it?"

"Not a word," said Deon. "But I knew they'd been an item for some time. Off and on."

"How was everyone else?"

"Fine. Just playin' cards. Anne sat between Eugene and the chief."

Max asked, "Where did you go after the game?"

"I went for a beer at a local bar."

"People see you?"

"Yeah, they'd back me," said Deon.

Max stood to leave. "Here's my card. Call if you think of anything else."

"Of course. Always willing to help the police," said Deon.

As Max retreated to the elevators, he began to see a clearer picture of Anne: a flirty, pretty girl from humble beginnings who couldn't help herself even if she tried, yet she had dedicated her life to helping others.

As Max left the waiting room behind, he imagined Nurse Anne Martin strolling out to greet visitors and leading them to the rooms of sick family members or post-op patients. He could see her holding someone's hand or helping a patient take a sip of water. He could see her comforting a patient in pain or listening while someone shared his or her darkest fear of imminent death.

Before Max left the hospital, he rode the elevator up to administration, which had cheery pastel-yellow walls, but it still had the hospital scent, just fainter, as if the smell had wafted up in the elevators or clung to the clothes of those who worked here.

Max asked a secretary who he could speak to in regards to a deceased nurse on the medical surgical floor. Max gave her Anne's name, took a seat, and waited.

A half hour later, he was about to complain, when a man and woman approached and greeted him. They escorted him to a small conference room.

The woman introduced herself as Mrs. Grimes, Vice President of Hospital and Health Services, and the man, as Mr. Rodriguez, the Chief Nursing Officer. Mrs. Grimes, a statuesque blonde with features perhaps chiseled by a plastic surgeon, because they seemed too perfect, extended a hand. "Sorry to keep you waiting, detective." Mrs. Grimes' gravelly voice did not match her delicate face.

Max took a seat. "I'm investigating the death of Anne Martin, and I just have a question or two."

"Of course. How can we help?" asked Mrs. Grimes. Despite the "we," Mr. Rodriguez, a short-statured man with a dark mustache, waited patiently. Max surmised he was either there as a second pair of ears, a witness in case of trouble, or was told to speak only if asked.

Max began, "As you know, we found Anne Martin dead beside Goldrush Creek. Were there any problems here at the hospital?"

Mrs. Grimes piped a response. "Yes, detective, but please keep it under wraps. We are conducting a full internal investigation of drug diversion. In fact, as soon as Mr. Rodriquez notified me of the problem, the board approved hiring an outside drug diversion expert to identify points of access and to recommend strategies for mitigation."

Max asked, "What kind of drugs have been stolen?"

Mrs. Grimes replied, "The kind that would sell on the street —opioids, Fentanyl, oxy, midazolam."

"How far back has the problem existed?" Max asked while jotting notes.

Mrs. Grimes folded her hands. "Mr. Rodriguez became aware of it a few months ago. We're still conducting our investigation."

"Has anyone in particular been identified as a suspect?" asked Max.

"No. Unfortunately, there are many shifts and many hands that have access." Mrs. Grimes nodded, giving permission for Mr. Rodriquez to speak up.

"Cases of drug diversion are in the news constantly. The DEA tracks pharmacies, even those in hospitals, doctors' prescriptions, and manufacturers. There was a recent case in one hospital of a nurse diverting drugs and taking needles she used on patients for her own use. In a larger case, two nurses stole excessive amounts of drugs—in that case, the DEA fined the hospital a couple million. Large or small, we will not tolerate drug diversion."

"I appreciate that, Mr. Rodriquez," said Max. "Is Dr. Grant on staff at this hospital?"

Mrs. Grimes' eyes shot wide, like his mentioning the name had sent a dagger right through her. "Thank you, Mr. Rodriquez. I'll take it from here. You may resume your duties."

Before he left, Mr. Rodriquez added, "For the record, Anne Martin was a great nurse. I can't imagine she had anything to do with stealing those drugs."

Mrs. Grimes waited for him to close the door. "I presume you mean Dr. Kenneth Grant?"

Max nodded.

"He's not on staff anywhere. He no longer has a medical license."

"You sound like you personally remember it. You were here then?" asked Max.

"Kenneth was a charming man. Still is. I see him racing around town in his little red Porsche. We were both so young then and climbing up in the world. I dated him for a while. You know how it is when you're young. Can't keep apart. But Kenneth had a drinking problem. I'd saved his bacon a couple of times, put him in a quiet room and an empty bed where he could sleep it off. He had his first DUI just after his thirtieth birthday. I don't know how he made it through med school. I knew he was a train wreck, so I broke up with him. By the end of the week, he was dating another nurse. His second DUI was a year later. The second time around, besides alcohol, he also had cocaine in his system. The medical board frowned on a second offense. I guess he figured the cocaine would offset the alcohol. Instead, the combination—"

Max finished her sentence. "Makes for an alert drunk. I've seen it firsthand. We learned that phrase in the police academy."

"With the second more serious offense, the medical board revoked Kenneth's license to practice. I think he started working for a pharmaceutical company—Kinsey, I believe."

"Thank you for your time, Mrs. Grimes. I appreciate your giving me this information. It might help." Max rose and turned to leave.

"Detective King."

Max turned back.

"Kenneth Grant, in the old days at least, well, he also had a temper. Somehow, I doubt that's changed."

"I'll keep that in mind."

"You don't think Anne's death had something to do with the diverted drugs, do you?" asked Mrs. Grimes.

"At this point, Mrs. Grimes, I know very little. I'm just following the bread crumbs."

As Max rode down the elevator and crossed the lobby, he wondered if Anne had dealt drugs on the black market? It could easily place her in danger. But had she become that desperate? Or had Grant pushed her into it? Or was Shane, the pharmacist, involved? Or Deon, the nurse?

8

Max located Dr. Grant by phone and asked to meet with him. Grant had been making his last call of the day, so he invited Max to meet him at his house.

Max pushed the intercom and the electric gate swung open. He drove up the hill on a private road and parked before a modern glass, stainless steel, and granite behemoth. The architecture told Max a lot about the man who lived inside—he was cold with hard edges.

Max rang the bell. He could see clear through the house from the glassed-in front entry through to a wall of windows in the living room that faced rolling golden hills and the valley below.

A maid with a Spanish accent answered the door and led Max through the great room. Max's shoes tapped lightly against the travertine floors. A white quartz fireplace reached up to the second story beside a catwalk with stainless steel railings. The decor was gray and black and white with acrylic tables and splashes of red.

Panoramic vanishing glass doors stood open to blend the inside and outside into one space. Max followed the maid outside, where an infinity pool cascaded, seemingly, into the valley below. White tables and chairs and gray chaise recliners faced the pool and the hills beyond.

A red hawk shot across the sky and swooped down, chasing a small bird.

Kenneth Grant sat under an umbrella, sipping iced tea with a lemon wedge and a sprig of mint. A clear acrylic tray contained a pitcher of tea, lemon wedges, mint sprigs, a white honey pot, and an empty glass, presumably for Max.

Grant didn't get up. He stared straight ahead through dark sunglasses.

"Thank you for seeing me." Max took a seat.

Grant brought a cigarette to his lips, inhaled a deep drag, and stubbed it out in a steel ashtray. "I want Anne's murderer caught too. What do you need?"

Max wondered if the refusal to meet him eye-to-eye meant asserting his dominance or attempting to avoid giving himself away.

Max asked, "Did you quarrel with Anne outside at Eugene's?"

"Anne needed a strong arm sometimes. She made a lot of mistakes. I was trying to help her," said Grant.

"And she resisted your 'guidance'?" Max felt tension rise in Dr. Grant as he invoked a sarcastic tone on the world "guidance." But Grant still refused to meet Max's gaze. The longer he avoided Max, the more suspicious Max became.

"Anne was her own worst enemy. A tragedy waiting to—"

Max interjected, "How about your mistakes, Dr. Grant?"

At this, Grant turned. He pulled off his sunglasses and bore his hazel eyes into Max's cold blue ones, "What are you talking about?"

"I mean the two DUIs that cost you your medical license."

At this, Grant relaxed. "Absolutely! Spot on, Detective King. Except that it was the best screw-up of my life. Probably even saved my life. Yes, I lost my license, because I *am* a drug and alcohol addict. It's never in the past. It lurks. It lives inside you and waits for one moment of weakness. I was young and arrogant, a real ass-hole. Screwed women. Abused cocaine and booze. I lived in the fast lane, and it all came crashing down. The first time, I hired a lawyer, took classes, polished my record, and the board reinstated me. But I thought I just needed to control it, to hide it better. That's how an addict talks to himself. A second time was inexcusable."

"And..." said Max, urging him to continue.

"I go at things full tilt. Always have. I mowed over people to get what I wanted. It was easy. But I had to mow over myself. I got help, and I faced my issues head on. No excuses. I've been sober just over ten years—until last night. Today, I start all over." Grant raised his tea and gulped it down.

"So other than a store clerk who sold you the bottle of vodka, you have no witnesses to your whereabouts last night? Where do you work Dr. Grant?"

"I'm a sales rep for Kinsey Pharmaceuticals."

Max's voice carried a tone of mild shock. "You handle drugs and you're an addict?"

"I don't handle any samples that could be abused. I have those shipped directly to my doctors." He took a large gulp of tea. "Anne's addiction was gambling. But she didn't want to stop. She lacked discipline. She always thought—as many do—that she could control the beast. Tame it. Well, you can't. I loved Anne, and yes, I was tough with her. I had to be or...or I'd lose her, but I lost her anyway."

"You fought with her outside at Eugene's? What about?"

"The usual. Money. I'd helped her before, and I made sure she always paid me back—every penny. Last night, she was giddy. Flirting and joking. She shot those greedy green eyes at Eugene. I like Eugene. I didn't want Anne to mess with him. He's been through enough. That's what I told her outside. Anne blew through her inheritance—God, how I tried to stop her! You don't give an addict drugs. And you don't give a gambling addict money."

"She had bruising at her jaw. Someone struck her? Was it you?"

"I could never..." Grant didn't finish. He jumped to his feet and ran his hands through his hair. "I don't remember! But I love her! I could never..." Grant gazed out at the valley and contemplated. "In recovery, you learn that addicts aren't supposed to partner with other addicts—it's too dangerous. But Anne and I—we understood each other like no one else could understand us. Anne had a sweet side, a loving side, a good side. So do I. We had happy moments, fun times. If we were out, she protected my sobriety. I'm surrounded by wineries, but I can't drink. And Anne needed to stop gambling."

Max listened carefully. It wasn't so much about hearing the answers to his questions as it was about hearing Kenneth Grant's perspective—understanding how this man saw the world and how he saw Anne. "Did you see Anne when you drove back to her house drunk?"

Grant paced. "I remember beating on her door and calling her name. The next thing I know, I woke up in my car."

Max jotted a note. *Alcohol-induced memory lapse.* "Did you know that drugs have gone missing from the hospital?"

Grant's anger flared. "My God, Anne! How could you?"

"We don't know that she did it."

"We don't know that she didn't."

"Did you kill her, doctor?"

Grant raged. "Get out! Get out of my house!"

"Looks like you have one other beast to control, doctor—your anger. One more question and I'll leave."

Grant bore his eyes into Max. His nostrils flared. He grit his teeth. His neck muscles tensed like sinew stretched so tight it would snap.

Max rose to his feet and glared back, knowing his final question would set Grant off even more. "Anne had sex last night. I'm guessing it wasn't with you?"

Dr. Grant grabbed a chair and hurled it over the embankment. He let out a guttural cry, like a man who had lost more than he could bear and he couldn't stand to lose any more. He sank to his knees. His shoulders heaved. His head dropped into his cupped hands.

Max let himself out. He knew that kind of rage. It could lead to murder—a sudden, instantaneous swing of impulse that sent a fist into a jaw or a rock smashing against a skull.

Had the trigger been Anne's attention to Eugene? Or had Dr. Grant simply put Anne in a box so small she had no other way out but to steal from the hospital? Did he hate Anne for being weak? Or did he hate himself for murdering her when she failed to follow his prescription?

Cynthia answered the door, somewhat surprised. "Shane? Come in."

Shane kissed Cynthia on the cheek. "I need to see Eugene."

"We just finished dinner. Have a seat. I'll bring you boys some dessert." In no time, Cynthia handed Shane and her father the remaining strawberry pie, and she settled into the floral sofa beside her father.

"Is something wrong?" asked Eugene.

"I'm not sure. I should have mentioned this to the police when they came to see me, but I didn't. I thought I'd get your opinion first." Shane winced and adjusted his body to find a pain-free position.

"What is it?" Eugene balanced the pie plate on his knees, careful to avoid getting crumbs on his shorts or white cotton shirt as he scooped a bite into his mouth.

Shane said, "Some months back, Anne hadn't been herself. I thought it was her break-up with Grant that had her gloomy."

"I remember. I also thought it was from the break-up," said Eugene.

"I joked around with her. Told her she looked like she'd seen The Ghost of Christmas Past, and she says, 'Shane, all of the ghosts have come home to haunt me.' Last night, I mentioned that she was all smiles again. I asked how she got rid of the ghosts. She said she'd taken a loan from a creep named A-gamer. But she said the chief had cleared it up. I think she slipped, because as soon as she said it, she begged me to keep it to myself."

Eugene stopped eating. "That doesn't sound like Anne at all."

Cynthia sniped, "You only see one side of her, father. The good side. But I love that about you."

Eugene's face flushed with disappointment. "What else did she say?"

"Nothing. She clammed up." Shane shoved another bite of pie into his mouth.

"Did Kenneth know about this?" asked Eugene before taking another bite.

"I don't think so," said Shane. "Anne said she promised the chief she wouldn't say a word. She said it was in the past."

Eugene set his empty plate on the coffee table. "Then I'm sure it was."

Shane swallowed his last bite and set down his plate. "Delicious. Thank you, Cynthia. Marry me. Take care of me like you take care of your father. I'll make you the happiest woman alive. And you'll make me the happiest man alive."

Cynthia scooped up the empty plates and carried them to the sink.

Eugene beamed a wide smile. "Excellent idea! I say we turn this sad day around. Please say yes, Cynthia. Nothing would make me happier. I'm not going to live forever. Enjoy the love that has eluded me all these years."

"But you need me, Papa," reminded Cynthia, returning to her seat.

Eugene put an arm around her. "Don't let that stop you. Shane can move in here. We've plenty of room. This will be yours one day. Oh, do consider it, Cynthia. Say yes if you love the man. I may have missed the boat, but you shouldn't."

Shane added, "I'll give up my job at the twenty-four hour pharmacy and help with your family business. Just say yes."

Cynthia's expression warmed. She blushed. "It would be all the merrier to have two men around here to care for. And Shane, I love you more than I've ever loved any man—you practically live here anyway. So, yes. I accept."

Shane threw a hand over his heart. "I'm a happy man, Cynthia!"

Eugene wrapped his arms tightly around his daughter's shoulders and kissed her on the forehead. "I'm happy for you both."

Cynthia wriggled out of her father's embrace. "This calls for a toast." She scurried to the kitchen.

Eugene said, "I can use help at work. We've become so busy lately."

Shane added, "I have an appointment with the surgeon. I've been putting off, but I'll be as fit as can be. Promise. And pain free, God willing."

Cynthia returned with three uncapped beers and passed them around. "It may not be champagne, but it's the thought that counts."

"A toast to you both. May you have many happy years!" Eugene tipped back the beer and drank a long draught.

"I'll just have a sip." Shane slowly rose to his feet, giving his back time to adjust. "I have a shift at the pharmacy tonight."

"Well, that's hours away," said Eugene. "What kind of a man is my daughter marrying?"

"A good man. To future happiness and prosperity!" Shane gulped down the entire beer. He set the empty bottle on the table. "So do you think I should tell the police, Eugene? About what Anne told me? I don't even know if it's true."

Eugene pondered quietly. "I suppose you should. It will either lead somewhere or not."

Cynthia walked Shane to the door. Shane set a gentle kiss on Cynthia's lips, which she returned, before blushing and gently pushing him away.

Shane smiled. "Your shyness is one thing I've always loved about you."

"You love my cooking," joked Cynthia, patting Shane's belly.

"I do love that too." Shane kissed her on the forehead. "You set the date. I'll start packing. I promise—we'll be happy. And with the two of us here, I think your father will be inspired to find a good woman for himself."

Cynthia glanced over her shoulder. "Papa deserves a good woman."

9

M ax should have skipped his last stop, as it was already six, and he had to be in his night class at seven. He told himself he needed to know the answer to one more question before the night ended.

Dr. Burton had held his seat last week, when he missed class due to his father's funeral. He presumed she would understand if he showed up late tonight, what with his job. Besides, the college wasn't too far away. In his undercover car, a silver Ford Taurus Interceptor, he could make it on time or close to it if he ran with lights and siren.

Max drove up the dirt driveway to Eugene's house. Shane Drake passed him going out. Why had he doubled back? Did they collude on a story? Or was Shane simply stopping by to see Cynthia?

Cynthia answered the door, somewhat flustered and blushing. She smoothed her apron. Max could smell beer on her breath. Cynthia didn't look the type, but Max knew to keep his net spread wide at this point—and that meant no presupposing.

"Detective King? Come in, please."

Three bottles of beer sat on the table. Shane must have had one. Cynthia cleared away the empty bottle.

Eugene set down his beer. "We're toasting Cynthia's engagement to Shane. It's a happy ending to a horrific day."

"Congratulations, Cynthia!"

"Thank you. Can I get you coffee or tea?"

"No, thanks. I'm good," said Max. "I need to speak to your father in private."

With anxious speed, Eugene popped up from his seat. "Let's go to my office."

"No need. I'm popping by the store." Cynthia kissed her father on the cheek. "Any requests?"

"Dried apricots, dear. We're all out. You know the ones I like," said Eugene. "I'll meet you at the mortuary later."

"See you there, Papa." Cynthia stripped off her apron, hung it on a wall hook, grabbed her floral purse, and headed out.

As soon as the front door closed, Max sat in the same armchair as before. "We know that Anne had sexual relations the night she died. Was it with you? The lab is running the DNA."

Eugene crumbled. He arched forward. His head fell into his hands. "Oh, dear. Oh, dear. I couldn't say a word this morning. Not in front of Cynthia. She may be my daughter, but she did not like Anne—well, that's not true—she liked her fine when she dated Kenneth."

"Walk me through the timeline," said Max.

Eugene fell back into the sofa like a defeated man. "Anne came by before the poker game. We had a drink. It's been a long time since I dated Mayleen. I was flattered. Anne is beautiful. And look at me—I know I'm not the kind of material that girls like her go for, but she confided in me. I could see Cynthia's disapproving glances as she worked in the kitchen. Game time crept up and guests started to arrive. I took a shot. When Cynthia answered the door, I suggested to Anne that she come back to the house after the others had left, and we could finish the conversation. She lit up. She seemed so relieved."

Although Max had questions, Eugene headed down a road of his own choosing. For now, Max nudged him along. Sometimes, if he stopped to listen, victims—and murderers—told him exactly what he needed to hear to solve a case. "She confided in you about what?"

"Her life. The mess she'd made of it by going for the wrong kind of guy. Hot-tempered guys with flashy cars like Kenneth Grant, instead of nice, stable fathers like me. She prattled on about having made some big mistakes. But she wanted to start over."

"Did she come on to you during the game?" asked Max.

Eugene blushed. "She paid attention to me, yes. But she flirted with others too. The chief. Shane. Even Chen, and he's married."

"How did Grant take it?"

"When we took a break, Grant insisted on having a word with her outside. Anne went. And while they were outside, Cynthia pulled me aside and gave me a royal scolding—my daughter scolded *me*, her father. She called Anne a 'floozy.' I'll bet you haven't heard that term in a while. Cynthia means well. She just didn't want me to get my heart broken again."

"And Anne came back to see you?"

"Yes, but she didn't want Kenneth to know, and I didn't want Cynthia to know, so I told Anne to wait about half an hour, so Cynthia would have gone to bed. It was silly! I'm a grown man, and I'm sneaking around in my own house. I let Anne in through the French doors to my bedroom. We...we spent time together. She poured out her heart, told me she owed the casino money. But she didn't care. She'd pay it back and she'd get help for her gambling problem. I couldn't hold back. I told her that I'd loved her for a long time, but I thought she loved Grant. Anne said she needed someone who wasn't like Grant."

"Did she fight with Grant last night?"

"I didn't see any fight. Anne could make every man at the table feel special. Kenneth didn't like it. He's protective. Jealous. Anne told me that he wanted to control her. I loved her. Do you think I'm foolish?"

Max didn't know how to begin to answer that question. So many questions flooded his mind. Had Anne pitted Dr. Grant against Eugene? Or had she hit bottom and decided to try a different kind of man? Was her speech to Eugene the real Anne Martin? Or did she just manipulate men to get what she wanted and Eugene was her next victim?

"I'm not the one to answer that question. Mr. Carter. At least you've loved a woman, a couple of them. I've not gotten that far yet. I mean, I'd like to find a woman to love. Some day."

"But you're young. I'm fifty-five this year. Ah, well, if anything good has come from this, it's Cynthia's engagement to Shane. He finds it hard to date, just like Cynthia. I think they'll be happy. I'm happy for them."

Max thought about his own father—never married. He'd always told Max he had married the badge, but Max didn't buy it. Plenty of women had flirted with him over the years, but none ever got close. Was David King just happy alone? By twenty-six, Max wondered the same thing about himself.

Eugene asked, "You won't tell Cynthia, will you?"

"I don't think she needs to know, Mr. Carter."

"Look, Detective King. We talked, and Anne kissed me, and...and...it was not just sex. We...we made love. Anne seemed so happy, so relieved to be with me. She knew that I would take care of her. We spoke of the future. I...I mentioned getting married. She cried in my arms. She told me everything. I told her once we were married, I'd pay off her loan to the casino, and we'd get her help. We'd both start over."

Max worked hard to keep a line of dissociation in place. Sometimes, it meant peering over the edge of a cliff without getting close enough to fall into the abyss like now—Max could not see what Eugene wanted him to see. A detective had to feel empathy, listen to cadences, and watch for truth and lies. He could not be completely dispassionate, but his perspective had to remain objective. The senses could be deceived.

Max believed Eugene's story, but Eugene wore rose-colored glasses when he gazed at Anne. Max needed to see all of her—colors and stripes and spots and chinks—if he stood a chance of finding her killer. "Thank you for your candor."

Max didn't blame Eugene for donning rose-colored glasses to view a perfect Anne Martin. But Max saw Eugene as the last in a line of dominoes. Eugene's losses of one woman after the other, followed by the beautiful Anne Martin in his bed, would blind any man. It didn't mean Anne had lied to him, but it did inform Max that Eugene could not be considered impartial. That didn't make him evil. It made him all the more human.

By finding Anne's killer, Eugene might come to know the truth of that night. But would he want to know? Was Anne looking for a chance to start over? Or a steady bankroll? Or had she finally, like Paul Lopez said, hit rock bottom and vowed to turn her life around? Or had Eugene felt used and betrayed. Had he felt sucker-punched, and he fought back, followed her, and killed her?

Max refrained from asking Eugene about the drugs that had gone missing, because, at this point, it could not be ascribed to Anne. Had Anne mentioned it, presumably Eugene would have mentioned it, since he knew about her casino debt. Maybe Anne hadn't stolen the drugs. Still, a single question emerged from the pack: Who killed her and why?

Eugene added, "There is one other thing you should know. This just came to my attention. That's why Shane was here. I don't care what Anne did in the past but it might help you."

"What is it?" asked Max.

"Shane informed me that Anne had confided in him that

she'd previously obtained money from someone named A-gamer. He also said that Chief Goldsby fixed the problem for her. I think that's why she didn't tell me, because the problem had been resolved. I hope that's why she didn't tell me."

"That's a pretty big accusation." Max remained calm on the exterior but his heart beat a little faster. He could not fathom the chief succumbing to Anne's charms and sticking his nose into this mess unless he had official clearance and backup.

"Shane thought so too, which is why he didn't say anything when you spoke to him this morning. He wanted my opinion. I said he should tell you."

"It's hearsay," said Max. "Anne told him this but she's dead?"

"Yes. Idle gossip at this point," said Eugene,

"I'm glad you mentioned it. I will follow up on it."

Eugene leaned forward. "Perhaps this is out of place. I hope not. I mean this sincerely. Please accept my deepest condolences for your father. We took care of him for the services. Crane Carter & Son Mortuary—that's me—the son. David King was the best chief of police Wine Valley has ever had. I'm very sorry for your loss."

Max pulled back from the edge. In this space, he had to maintain a well-defined line and not cross it. He did sense that Eugene was sincere, rather than implying any untoward connection between them that would impede the investigation.

"Yes, well, that subject is off topic, given that I'm here in an official capacity, Mr. Carter. But thank you. My partner and Kate Wolf, my godmother, helped me with those details."

"Of course. That's quite normal."

Max showed himself out. He had no sooner left and hopped into his car than his phone rang.

"Captain? You're working late," said Max.

"You sittin' down?"

"I am, as a matter of fact. I just re-interviewed Eugene. He was Anne's mysterious lover."

"Well, while you ponder that, ponder this, 'cause that's not the kicker."

Despite the tension, Max loved how Jayda—now Captain Banks—could string out a good story. She once took twenty delicious minutes to reach a punch line, and she knew he'd wait. "You've got my attention, Captain."

"The prints found on the cigar cutter near the crime scene belong to Chief Goldsby. He just left my office, and he's havin' kittens. Says he's bein' framed."

While Captain Banks' tone remained completely professional, Max knew her well enough to hear the subtle thread of twisted pleasure in her voice.

Max asked, "Relieved of duty?"

"Not yet. It's circumstantial. But the mayor just called me. She's on her way over to see me—what a time to get a promotion."

"I'd love to be there, but I'm on the way to school."

"10-4. You are 10-7 this evening." Banks gave the code for "out of service." She added, "I will never stop an officer from obtaining a good education, Max. That's your daddy's policy, and I'm keeping it."

"That sounded just like David King."

"I'll take that as a compliment."

Max confirmed, "You should."

As Max drove down the lane, his heart pounded. Chief of Police Frank Goldsby—a suspect in a murder case? Max let his faint smile fade. Even if the chief did have a reason to want Anne dead, Max owed him a thorough investigation.

Max needed to re-interview Shane Drake and speak to the chief. And Eugene—what to make of him? His story of love and passion and Anne wanting to turn corners could just as easily be one of anger and retribution and murder.

Killers were pros at psychology—which was why Max had signed up for Dr. Burton's class in forensic psychology in the first place. Anne might have been a lousy gambler but the best player of men at the table.

Max remembered his father's warning after he'd caught Max, about ten years old then, playing with a hornets' nest: "Son, you play with a hornets' nest, they'll swarm you like flies to honey, and they won't quit until each one has sunk its stinger into your flesh and pumped in poison. If you live, you'll wish you hadn't." Max felt the same way now. But it was his job to stir the nest and agitate the killer until he exposed himself.

Should the killer turn and attack him? He'd be ready.

By the time Shane opened the back door to let in the night air, he felt woozy. He blamed the beer, even though it should not have been a problem in combination with the meds he'd taken that day. He decided to take a short nap.

He set his phone alarm and placed the device on the nightstand. He stripped off his clothes, jumped into his Padres pajama pants, and tumbled into bed, flopping on his belly under the covers. His cheek sank into the pillow, his eyes closed, and he gently snored.

A figure slipped in through the back door, crossed through the kitchen, and headed to the bathroom. A gloved hand reached for the box of Fentanyl patches in the medicine cabinet.

The visitor snuck into Shane's bedroom and sat on the bed beside a snoring Shane.

Fingers peeled back the covers. They dove into the box and pulled out an envelope, ripped it open, peeled the protective covering from the back, and stuck the clear patch to Shane's lower back. One patch. Two. Three.

Hands plugged in the heating pad that lay on the floor beneath the wall plug. When warm, the hands set the pad over the patches on Shane's back and pressed gently to warm Shane's back.

Shane moaned.

Fingers gripped the covers and lifted them up over Shane's shoulders. The same hands lit the butt of a cigar. Smoke curled in the air.

Shane's eyes popped open, but his pinpoint pupils could not focus. In a euphoria of dreams, free from pain, he inhaled a deep breath and let out a final exhalation. His heartbeat slowed, and slowed, and stopped.

10

Max settled into an aisle seat midway down the theater-styled rows in the Price-Wellsman Academy, an east-coast university specializing in sociology, psychology, forensics, police procedures, and criminology with satellites in several states, including California and Virginia, the latter known for training programs designed specifically for FBI profilers.

Semi-circular rows of seats faced a stage, a single-step platform, on which stood a black lectern and, beyond that, massive whiteboards covered the back wall. The room had sound-proof beige walls and fluorescent lighting. Students spilled in and settled into their seats.

Max had known from the start that he wanted to be a detective, to solve crimes like his father. As soon as Max graduated from high school and finished his bachelor's in criminology, he entered the police academy. It took another few years, working alongside then Lieutenant Banks, to train and transform from a rookie to an adept police officer before becoming eligible to take the detective's exam.

Meantime, Max read book after book and took on-line

classes in forensics, computer fraud, and criminal psychology, anything that could help him understand the criminal mind.

Dr. Beatrice Joy Burton entered the stage from a side door on the right. She wore navy blue slacks, a white shirt, and a silky, knee-length blue jacket that fluttered behind her as she walked. She set some papers on the lectern.

Max pulled up the tiny writing desk that dangled at the side of the chair, opened his leather-bound notebook, and poised his pen over the page, eager to take notes.

Dr. Burton moved slowly, methodically. Her jet-black hair skimmed her shoulders, and her black brows seemed like night to his day. He remembered her eyes when he had met her at his father's funeral: dark brown, but so dark they almost seemed black, like the eyes of a reptile. Her red lipstick was a bit stark for his tastes, especially against her skin—like the color of wheat on a summer day, which somehow added a soft touch to her otherwise edgy, gothic appearance, perfectly suited to the grisly subject matter of forensic psychology.

Dr. Burton faced the audience. "You are here because of Dr. Edmond Locard, French criminologist. His nickname was the 'Sherlock Holmes of France,' and you've probably heard his basic tenant: 'Every contact leaves a trace.'" With the push of a button on a remote in Dr. Burton's hand, a screen dropped down from the ceiling. With the push of another button, a passage flashed on the screen. Dr. Burton read it aloud to the class. Her voice resonated with each word:

"Wherever he steps, whatever he touches, whatever he leaves, even unconsciously, will serve as silent witness against him. Not only his fingerprints or his footprints, but his hair, the fibers from his clothes, the glass he breaks, the tool marks he leaves, the paint he scratches, the blood or semen he deposits or collects. All of these and more bear mute witness against him. This is evidence that does not forget. It is not confused by the excitement of the moment. It is not absent because human witnesses are. It is factual evidence. Physical

evidence cannot be wrong, it cannot perjure itself, it cannot be wholly absent. Only human failure to find it, study it, and understand it can diminish its value. –Dr. Edmond Locard."

Dr. Burton pushed a button on the remote, and the screen disappeared. She left the remote on the podium, stepped around it, and stood before the class. "Locard started the first police laboratory in 1910 in two attic rooms in a police facility in Lyon, France. He had to beg the police to give him the space. In his lifetime, he met Sir Arthur Conan Doyle, who penned the fictitious Holmes cases, but your cases are not fictitious. Your bodies are not characters in a novel. They lived and they died. And it's up to you to find their killers and bring justice to the dead. Since Locard's time, we've come to understand more about the criminal mind, the triggers and patterns and histories that forge human beings into killers..."

Max remained mesmerized for the entire three-hour class, which had one twenty-minute break halfway through, when he stepped out to stretch his legs. It had been a long day, but a Coke and a Snickers bar from the vending machines fueled him to the end.

Dr. Burton moved back and forth across the stage with ease. She spoke with passion and authority, captivating Max with case studies, her interviews with serial killers or other criminals, and descriptions of her own work in aiding the San Diego PD with cracking a case or making an arrest.

Max had done his homework on Dr. Burton. She was Max's age, but she was something of a genius. She finished high school at fifteen in San Diego, completed a double-bachelors in sociology and psychology with a minor in math, and earned a Ph.D. in Criminal Psychology from Yale. She then attended the FBI Academy in Quantico, Virginia. She worked for the FBI for a few months, before quitting the bureau and returning to San Diego, where her father lived. She taught classes, consulted with various police departments, and worked as a hostage negotiator for the SDPD.

The moment the lecture ended with a reminder to download the syllabus and stay on-track with the reading assignments, the crowd—about three-fourths men and one-fourth women— dispersed. Max's father would have liked better female numbers, but they had improved over time, in part due to David King, who volunteered to lecture in the after school criminal science program at the high school to encourage girls, like Jayda, to join the force.

After class, a few eager students rushed up to Dr. Burton with questions, but she kept shooting glances at Max while she answered them.

The only encounter Max and Dr. Burton had experienced prior to tonight had occurred after his father's funeral, when he saw her standing on a grassy hill. They spoke briefly.

Max recognized her after she'd already walked away from him—or he thought he had. The memory of a dark-haired childhood companion erupted from the black lake in his mind. David King had adopted Max when three and a half years old. Max knew little, other than that. But he vaguely remembered a dark-haired female playmate.

When the last student left, Max approached Dr. Burton.

"Hi, Max. I'm glad you made it," she said.

"Me too." Max had an important question to ask her, but asking someone—"Were you my childhood friend, and did you kill a kitten? Because all I remember is you holding a dead kitten"—was awkward, to say the least. As much as Max wanted to rush in, his training told him to be smart. That sounded simple, but restraining his curiosity demanded extreme discipline. Although his hairstyle—buzzed on the sides and longish on top—attested to the fact he sometimes handed the reins to the impulsive, *this-is-the-very-best-idea-you've-ever-had* Max, and he paid the price for it—like with the haircut.

Dr. Burton broke the silence. "I read about Anne Martin. How's the case going?"

"Good. It's moving along," said Max.

"I hear Chief Goldsby is on the list of suspects. That must be interesting for you," said Joy.

Max wondered where she'd gotten her information. "I can neither confirm nor deny your statement." He liked his pat answer. He'd become used to not divulging information.

Still, Max's brain worked overtime. The WVPD's public relations liaison had managed to leave Goldsby's name out of the paper, so far, and had provided only a rudimentary description of Anne Martin as a local nurse, who may have had a tragic accident.

Joy whispered, "Here's a bit of top-secret information." She peered around as if to make sure the coast was clear. "My father was not a fan of Frank Goldsby."

Max whispered back, "Nor mine. You've been here a couple of weeks, and you have insider information. Maybe you did it."

Joy laughed. It was a childish laugh, the first break he'd seen in her otherwise serious demeanor. "Maybe. Cast your net wide, my father would say."

"Funny. My father said that too."

Joy's eyes narrowed and she cocked her head to the side as if scrutinizing him. "Did he?"

"Must be common," said Max.

"Right. Let me know if you need more time to catch up on last week's reading."

"Hey, I know you're some kind of genius, but I can read. I'll catch up fast."

Joy turned on her heels to leave. "Don't you dare read fast! Reading for meaning means you read slowly, methodically, no different than reading a crime scene."

"Well, actually, there's a big difference. A lot less blood," quipped Max.

With a wink and a smile, Dr. Burton sailed through the door and off stage.

Max should have been tired when he got home, but the lecture had fired him up—or perhaps the Coke and Snickers bar had kicked in. He cracked open the textbook and began to read.

Max woke up to the sound of his phone ringing. He found himself stretched out on the red and yellow plaid sofa with a book sprawled across his chest and one leg dangling. Morning sunlight slapped him awake as effectively as a cold shower. The red and yellow plaid sofa assaulted his senses. "Dang, this is not a good pattern to wake up to. Sorry, Dad, but we need some new décor."

As Max struggled to sit up, he envisioned the fuel that it would take to blast his eyes open—a huge, strong coffee and two glazed donuts. He needed more sugar than crumble donuts could provide. He had no real knowledge of which donut had the higher sugar content. He went by feel. Crumble donuts, as good as they were, seemed too refined for some mornings— after all, they crumbled—but biting into a giant, airy, fried pastry, with so much sugar it dripped around the sides—a donut that, if he wanted to, and sometimes he did, he could shove whole into his mouth—gave him a mental can-do blast of energy.

He sincerely hoped the ringing phone would stop once someone realized they'd dialed the wrong number, but he knew better and grabbed it. "King here."

The chief's deep voice pounded against Max's eardrum. "Sure, chief. I'll be right there." Max checked his watch. The chief was in early. Real early.

Max needed a shower, but the chief sounded impatient, so

he threw on a clean white polo shirt over yesterday's pants and raced out the door.

The approved detective dress code varied widely from county to county. Some departments insisted on standard uniforms and ties, others on plain clothes, but Wine Valley's dress code allowed him to wear a polo shirt with police insignia —white, navy, or black shirts with gold logos—and a suit jacket, when needed. His department found that casual attire worked better than uniforms for detectives needing to extract information from witnesses, due to the lower intimidation factor.

In this instance, the only danger to Max was the chief, and knowing he'd done nothing to deserve Goldsby's caustic wit, indignation, or rebukes offered little solace.

11

On the way to the precinct, Max called Kinsey Pharmaceuticals and spoke to a human resources representative who confirmed Dr. Grant's story. He'd been a model employee. Max didn't necessarily buy it. The guy as much as admitted addicts will lie—to themselves and to others. Did Grant have an angle? Was he diverting drugs to people outside of Kinsey?

Next, Max called Captain Banks and asked her to assign someone to dig into the doctor's finances and Shane Drake's. Kinsey Pharmaceuticals might pay Grant well, but was it enough to live large like he did? Or maybe he'd scored big at gambling and knew to leave well enough alone, unlike Anne. Either way, Max needed to make sure it added up. Dr. Grant had the most knowledge about drugs, along with Shane and Deon. Were they diverting drugs? What did Anne know that got her killed?

Shane didn't live large. But he might just be smart enough to lay low if he sold drugs. He certainly used them.

Despite the extra time it took, Max rushed into the donut shop on Stagecoach Street, a place he and his father had frequented, which was perhaps the reason he loved donuts: they came with irreplaceable memories of good times with his father.

Max grabbed his sugar fix, parked Baby Blue, his Mustang convertible, in the parking garage, and sprinted to the chief's office. He needed to ask the chief some tough questions. Before he could prove the man innocent—he had to know in what ways he was guilty.

Max finished chewing and swallowing the first donut as he knocked on the chief's door. He heard the chief's voice. "Come in." The second donut would have to wait. He kept the bag clutched in his hand and opened the door.

The chief's office had that newly painted and carpeted smell, but the chief hadn't yet settled in like Captain Banks. Boxes sat in stacks against the wall. But that was not what caught Max's eye. The chief had company.

Joy turned to greet him. "Hello, Max. You look like crap."

Max felt completely disheveled as he slipped into the chair next to Dr. Burton. "I feel like crap, Dr.Burton. I was up late doing homework."

In gray slacks and a silky black shirt, Dr. Burton had a polished presentation. Her button-front blouse with three-quarter cuffed sleeves gave her dark hair and eyes competition for attention. She wore a black pearl necklace and earrings that screamed, "Oh, these—just casual black pearls from the seas of China." Somehow, the jewelry seemed like a gift, not something she would have selected for herself, since she rubbed an earlobe as if an earring annoyed her.

Max asked, "Chief...what's going on here?"

"I'm a suspect in a goddamn murder investigation, that's what's going on here!" spewed Goldsby. The veins on his neck stuck out and his cheeks flushed red, which made his white hair all the whiter. "I just hired Dr. Burton as a consultant on the case. She's your new partner. She's got a nose like her father. She's helped a few PDs crack cases."

Max had heard one word. He repeated it. "Partner?"

The chief's bloodshot eyes widened. He had lost sleep. "My cigar cutter with my fingerprints was found at the scene of a murder—that's not a good thing. I didn't do it, Max. Where's the case?"

Until Max was restricted from talking to the chief or the chief was taken into custody, Max had no reason not to share information. "I've interviewed Eugene and his daughter, Cynthia, as well as Shane Drake and Dr. Grant. Anne doubled back and slept with Eugene before walking home."

"Anne and Eugene?" The chief's face puckered like he'd eaten sour grapes. "What the—oh, never mind. Go ahead." The chief folded his arms over his bulging belly, as if to constrain himself from interrupting again.

Max continued, "Dr. Grant has anger issues. He says he loves Anne, but she confided in Eugene that he was too controlling. Anne supposedly broke it off with Grant. She flirted with Eugene at the poker party."

Goldsby nodded. "That's true, but Anne flirting with the boys is not uncommon. She keeps it lively. No harm. No foul."

Max added, "So I've heard. Grant says he was trying to help Anne with her gambling addiction. Anne owed money to the casino." The chief's eyes diverted to his desk, but otherwise, he maintained a poker face. Was he waiting for a full briefing or had he known about Anne's gambling problem? Max continued, "I have some new information that supposedly came from Shane Drake, so I need to interview him again to verify it." Max leaned in. "Chief, um, I'm just doing my job, so don't take this the wrong way. I gotta ask. Did you have relations with Anne?"

"That's none of your business!" barked the chief.

"Chief," said Joy, leaning forward and using a soft

monotone to grab his attention and to put him at ease. "Answer the question. It's off-the-record, right, Max?"

Max didn't know if he quite agreed with that, but he let it slide. "Sure. Off-the-record at this point, chief. You know the saying—it's better to tell us now than tell a dozen jurors later."

"Oh, God. I can't believe this is happening. No, we didn't. She kissed me after I helped her. That's it." The chief rubbed his hands over his face, as if to wipe away the incriminating memory.

Max asked, "Do you know a loan-shark named A-gamer?"

The chief jumped up from his chair and trudged back and forth. After a couple of laps, he leaned over, placed his palms flat on his desk, and glared at Max. "How do you know about that? No one knew about that! I didn't really do anything. Nothing illegal."

Joy intervened. Max noticed that her calm tone brought the chief down out of the rafters. "Chief, no one is judging you. Just tell us what happened. It could lead us to Anne's real killer. And exonerate you."

"You're right. Maybe it was A-gamer. I forgot all about that punk-ass drug dealer." The chief sank into his chair. "If this gets out, I'm ruined." The chief shook his head and let out a deep sigh before dropping his shoulders, a suppliant sinner ready to confess. "Anne was foolish. When the casino cut her off, she borrowed five grand from A-gamer, thinking she could turn around her losing streak. It was a mistake. She'd been paying him off regular, but A-gamer kept raising the interest. She'd never get out. She was scared. Real scared. She told me she won some money at a game in Riverside. She had enough to pay off the balance."

The chief clasped his hands before him. "I went with her to see A-gamer. She made me wait outside. For my protection, she said—so we weren't seen together. When she came out, I was supposed to go in and talk to A-gamer. But I got antsy. I walked in. When she saw me, she hightailed it out of there. I went over to A-gamer and told him that her account was closed, permanently, and that if he loaned her another penny or asked her for another penny, I'd find him and put his punk ass behind bars for so long, he'd need a set of dentures when he got out."

Max asked, "Chief, did you know that drugs have gone missing from the hospital where Anne worked?"

The chief's cheeks flushed red. His head fell like dead fruit dropping from a tree. His eyes pleaded with Max and Joy. "Hell no, I didn't know! Damn it! Maybe Anne was trying to pay off A-gamer with stuff as valuable as cash. Maybe she didn't win a game in Riverside. You gotta believe me, I had nothing to do with it. And I didn't kill her! After the pay off, we came back to my place. Anne literally twirled in circles in my living room. She was giddy. She said, 'I'm free. I'm free. You saved my life, you brave knight.' I stepped in and we danced around the room. She kissed me. That's it."

Joy said, "Thanks for being candid, chief. It helps. We'll figure this out. Right, Max?"

"Right," said Max.

As Max and Joy left the chief's office, Max offered Joy his second glazed donut. "Need some sugar? That's to be taken literally."

"Max, those things will kill you."

Max pulled the donut from the bag and bit into it. He moaned in audible enjoyment. Max mumbled, "Trust me. Right now, this donut is saving my life."

Max knocked on Shane Drake's door. No one answered. He flipped through his booklet and called the number where Shane worked. "This is Detective King. Is Shane Drake there?"

"He never showed up for work," said a clerk. "I've been trying to call him all night."

Max and Joy walked the perimeter of the house. Max found the back door ajar. He signaled for Joy to wait. He withdrew his Glock, aimed, and entered the premises.

Max stepped inside. "Shane!" No answer.

Max cleared each room before entering the master bedroom. Shane lay on his stomach, a blanket over him. A cord ran from a wall socket to under the covers. Max holstered his gun and felt for a pulse. There was none. Shane was dead.

"Clear!" shouted Max, already donning plastic gloves.

Max handed Joy a pair of gloves as she entered the bedroom. Joy slid them on, knelt down, and stared into Shane's ashen face, blue lips, and fixed eyes. "What happened to you, Shane? Tell me."

Max thought it odd that Joy spoke to the corpse like an old friend, but then he realized he had been speaking to Anne Martin too. "If only he could. Our jobs would be way easier."

Max called for a team, which arrived within the hour. After technicians snapped pictures and collected evidence, Angelo removed the covers to get a better look at the body.

Max introduced Joy as a consultant. "Dr. Joy Burton, this is Angelo, the king of MEs"

"Doctor?" asked Angelo.

"Forensic psychology," said Joy.

Angelo's gray eyes shot wide with respect. "I dissect the body. You dissect the mind."

Joy gazed at Shane. "So true. Although, his mind can't talk. You'll have to talk for him."

"That's what I do," said Angelo.

Max observed the room. "No fight. And there doesn't appear to be forced entry, so he either died here alone or he knew his attacker. The back door off of the kitchen was unlocked. Any clues?"

"That's a lot of Fentanyl patches on his back," said Joy, eyeing the box on the nightstand. She peered inside the box. "Looks like there's one left, and the box contains five."

"I agree," said Angelo. "No contusions. Possible overdose, but we'll need toxicology to confirm it."

Max asked, "Accidental?"

"Three patches, probably not," said Angelo. "He's a big guy, but Fentanyl is a strong narcotic. One of these patches is usually worn for a couple of days. Could be two are old."

Joy added, "And he had a heating pad over them."

Angelo gave an impressed nod. "Exactly."

"What does that mean?" asked Max.

Angelo gestured using his gloved hands. "Warming the skin opens the pores, and that lets the narcotic in faster. I'll have to test the patches, but if they're all new, and if he had any other drugs or alcohol in his system, this may be death by overdose."

"Or murder by overdose," corrected Joy.

Max smelled a familiar smokey scent. He walked around the bed. On the floor, next to the nightstand, he saw a brown, stubbed, oblong shape on the carpet.

"A cigar blunt." Max grabbed an evidence bag and carefully scooped up the cigar butt. He recognized the scent—the chief's cigars. He wanted to be wrong. The chief might be a jerk, but was he a murderer? Or was someone out to frame him?

12

As the elevator ascended to the floor that held the chief's office, Max said, "You tell him. He likes you."

"He doesn't like me. He needs me," remarked Joy.

"I've changed my mind. I'll tell him. Then it's my treat for lunch," said Max.

Joy turned to Max. "Is the impish grin on your face about lunch or breaking the news to the chief of finding possible evidence linking him to second crime scene? For all we know Shane liked cigars too."

Max grinned and let out a sigh of satisfaction. "Both. We take the gifts life offers us, Joy."

"That we do, Max."

Once ensconced in the chief's office, Max asked, "Chief, where were you last night?"

The chief asked, "Is this still off-the-record?"

Neither Max nor Joy answered. They remained standing.

The chief rolled his eyes, "Fine. I was home alone. Why are you asking?"

"I found a cigar butt at—" Max was cut off by the door flying open.

Two men in suits and two uniformed officers stormed in.

Max knew the look—Internal Affairs. One of the suits said, "Chief, we're taking you in for questioning."

"Max! Joy! Find the killer. I swear—I'm innocent!" said the chief as they hauled Goldsby out the door and down he hallway.

Joy observed Max's face, which had a cherubic glow. "Why, Max, I do believe you're gloating."

Max gave her his most devilish smile and kept his eyes glued to the chief's back. "I've dreamt of this moment—and worse."

"Hmmm. Then you do have a dark side. I'm glad." Joy followed Max's gaze. "Enjoy every second of it. The case will wait."

Max took Joy to Belle's Burgers and Brew for lunch. He ordered shakes for them both—chocolate for him, strawberry for her.

Joy didn't object. She nibbled on a salad.

Max bit into his Western bacon cheeseburger and checked out in pure food-bliss. Moans and groans of pleasure slipped from his lips.

Belle popped by to visit. The septuagenarian wore her gray hair pulled back in a long braid that ran down her back. She had a strong face with prominent Native American cheekbones and fierce brown eyes. She wore blue cotton pants with a pale blue T-shirt, and over that, a white canvas apron with the title of her restaurant. Her tennis shoes were nothing fancy and well-worn. "Max, good boy, you have a date? Hi, I'm Grandma, Belle."

"His grandma?" asked Joy, taking a sip of her shake.

"No, darlin', everybody's grandma. Been here since the dinosaurs roamed."

"Nice to meet you, Belle. I'm Joy. This is one amazing shake."

"Lot'sa cream in that ice cream—none of that ice-milk, yogurt, low-sugar crapola."

Joy's smile widened.

Max recognized the look on Joy's face. It was how he felt sitting here—it was home. Joy didn't have the full-on "this is my hometown" grin, but a twinkle of "this could be my hometown" flashed in her eyes.

Belle studied Joy's face. "You were here the day of David King's funeral. And before that with your daddy as a young girl. I remember your dark hair and eyes."

Joy pushed her hair back behind her ears like a child who'd been caught spying on the Christmas tree to catch Santa in the act. "Sam passed away. He left me a house here. So you'll be seeing more of me."

Belle offered her condolences. "I'm sorry to hear that. I'm happy we'll be seeing' more of ya though, suits me just fine—and Max, here, well, it's nice to see him with female company that ain't work-related."

Max swallowed hard and raised a hand. "This is work-related. Belle, you're not helping me here. You're making me sound pathetic."

Belle said, "Max, you are pathetic, but in a good way—that's the new talk, ain't it—you just tack on 'in a good way' onto every insult."

Joy laughed so loudly, she threw a hand up to stop herself. "Yes, Belle, it is—and in a good way."

"Oh, man, I'm being ganged up on." Max shoved a couple of fries in his mouth. "And not in a good way, thank you very much."

"So, Max, is it murder or mayhem today?" Before Max could answer, Belle explained, "I like to know what's goin' on in my town, and Max, well, this boy's lips are tighter 'n a bad face lift."

"Belle!" pleaded Max.

Belle ignored him. "So we play a game. I ask him 'murder or mayhem?' because telling me that much doesn't break any laws."

Joy said with a twinkle in her eye. "Murder, Belle. Beauty and a beast."

Belle nodded her appreciation. "Thank you, darlin'. Welcome to Wine Valley. Your meal's on me. Max, I'll bring your bill."

Max threw up his hands. "She doesn't like me anymore. She used to like me, but now she likes you." He realized after he said it how childish it sounded.

"Max, no matter how young or how old, we goddesses stick together."

"Oh, I see. Goddesses. Hmmm. My dad gave me great advice. Know what he'd say right now. 'Son, you gotta rein in this horse before it runs over the cliff.' So I'm letting the goddess question burning in my brain go—like what makes a woman a goddess? I'm sticking to murder—it's much easier to solve than women."

Joy leaned over, snatched a couple of Max's French fries, and noshed them down. "And that, Max, is why you're going to be a great detective. Of course, we have yet to solve this case."

"Careful, Joy. Those will kill you."

"There are so many ways to die, Max." Her monotone voice and deadpan face gave him a sudden chill.

Max didn't know what to make of Dr. Joy Burton. His detective brain fired multiple warnings and questions. There were lots of missing pieces. But he didn't want to tip his hand. Not yet. He'd observe her a while longer. "Let's go talk to the Chens. They are low on my list of suspects, but that doesn't mean they didn't kill Anne or Shane or see something. Then we'll visit A-gamer."

Max and Joy stepped into the Chen's flower shop, ironically located on Flower Street, within the Vineyard Mall complex, a spider web plan with a central hub of megastores, like Walmart, Costco, and Macys, surrounded by a ring road with offshoots to restaurants, theaters, hobby shops, gyms, and more.

Max noticed the drop in temperature right away. He welcomed the chilled air that brushed against his face. A refrigerated display case burgeoned with colorful bouquets. The sweet-scented air gave Max a respite from the sweltering heat outside. He and Joy approached the counter. Mr. Chen and his wife worked together to construct a flower arrangement for a female customer who punched keys on her cell phone while she waited for her order.

Mr. Chen had thinning black hair and his wife, straight silver hair. They moved with synchronized ease: he gathered up the cellophane; she tied it with a ribbon. He gathered up the stem bits and placed them in the trash; she fiddled with the ribbon until it was a perfect bow.

Max and Joy paced the room until the customer left with her arrangement in-hand. They approached the counter. Max flashed his credentials. "I'm Detective Max King, and this is Dr. Joy Burton, special consultant. We're investigating the murder of Anne Mart—"

"Murder!" blurted Mr. Chen.

Mia put her fingers to her lips. "Eugene called. Said Anne was dead. Never said murder."

Joy offered an explanation, "We didn't have the autopsy report then." She nodded to Max to carry on.

Max sighed. "I'm afraid I have more bad news. Shane Drake was found dead this morning, possible overdose. We're not sure."

Lee and Mia stared at one another with wide-eyed bewilderment. Mia asked, "Are we in danger?"

Joy maintained a calm, soothing voice. "There's no reason to suspect you're in any danger. The two deaths are completely different."

Mia waved her hand. "Gambling is no good. Bring trouble. Bring bad luck."

Max asked Mr. Chen, "What can you tell us about the night of the poker game?"

Lee frowned. "Same as always. I left early as always. They play too late. Play late, get tired. Get tired, make mistakes. Make mistakes, lose money."

Mia patted him on the arm and scolded, "Don't play at all. Lose even less."

The synchronicity between them had been broken.

Joy asked, "How did you get involved with the poker game?"

Lee explained, "Eugene made us successful when we came to Wine Valley. Mortuaries and flowers—natural combination. He gives us steady business."

Mia waved a dismissive hand in the air and disappeared into the back room.

Lee let out a heavy sigh. His head hung low. "Mia is not upset at poker. She is upset that our daughter ran away—again. But that is not Eugene's fault. Mayleen, she made friends with a tough crowd in high school. Drug crowd. She ran away with a loser boyfriend to Los Angeles. We only heard from her when she wanted money. But she had money for tattoos." He wagged an angry finger. "We give her no money."

"When did she date Eugene?" asked Max.

Lee scowled. "Three years ago, Mayleen walked into our shop. Say she want to change. Done with bad crowd. Sorry, she say. Forty-two and want to change. I don't buy it, but Mia, she buy it. Mayleen worked in the shop, delivered flowers. She meet Eugene. He ask to marry her. She accept."

Max asked, "You didn't approve of the match?'

Lee's eyes shot wide. "No! Good match!" He drew out the word "no" for emphasis. "Eugene was happy. Mayleen was happy. We, happy. Then Eugene called me. Mayleen left Eugene a note and left town. Not one word after that. Drugs. She loves drugs more than Eugene. More than us!" Lee spit when he said it. While an accidental spray, it seemed more like he was frothing at the mouth in anger.

"And Anne?" Max directed the conversation back to the present case. "What can you tell us about her?"

Lee peered behind him to make sure his wife was out of earshot. He whispered. "Anne and Kenneth—bad match. No good." He wagged his finger again. "When Deon and I left Eugene's house, Grant and Anne are outside arguing. They stopped when they saw us and go back inside."

"Do you know what they argued about?" asked Joy.

"Anne tell him that he is not her keeper. Say they are over. He called her names I will not repeat."

"Anything else unusual?" asked Joy. "What about Deon?"

Mr. Chen shrugged. "Friend of Anne's. No good with cards. Tell us he plays video poker. Not the same. He lose his money fast, leave when I did."

"And the chief?" asked Max.

"He got good cards." Lee shrugged. "But when I left, Anne was winning."

Joy asked, "And Shane?"

Lee shrugged. "Good player. He walked around sometimes when his back hurt."

Max asked, "Does Shane smoke cigars?"

Lee shrugged. "Not that I see."

Max handed Mr. Chen his card. "If you think of anything, no matter what, give me a call."

Mr. Chen took the card. "Do you have children?"

"Need a wife first," joked Max.

Joy held up two empty palms.

Chen scowled. "Get no respect. They break your heart."

"Give Mayleen time," said Joy. "She came back before."

Max added, "She may have felt pressured to marry Eugene to keep you happy, but she couldn't tell you."

Mr. Chen frowned. "Bah! Bad seed stay bad seed. No turn into good seed."

13

E very town has its ugly side, its dark recesses, its
underbelly, and Wine Valley had its dark corners, shady
characters, and dive bars.

Max had pulled up A-gamer's record and located his choice
hangout: a bar called The Stinky Mule. The bar sat in a cheap
part of town, surrounded by a vintage brick-faced auto repair
shop with a sign that simply read "Garage," a small grocery
store, a liquor store, a hardware store, a day-old bakery, and
several empty stores in need of tenants.

The Stinky Mule had a façade reminiscent of the Old West.
A painting of a blue mule graced the wall to the left of the black
door of the entrance. The mule hee-hawed as he lifted his tail
to expel gas.

Max and Joy entered the establishment. It had no front
windows.

Even in daylight, darkness enveloped the room the moment
Max and Joy stepped inside and the door closed behind them.
Neon signs advertised beers and other alcoholic beverages, but
did little to light the faces of a couple of patrons hunched over
the bar.

Max's eyes began to adjust. The bartender, wiping a glass with a towel, did nothing to acknowledge them.

One area stood out. Green glass shades with bright white bulbs hung over two pool tables, where a motley group of boys, mostly white, laughed, drank, and played.

Max strolled toward the tables with Joy beside him. He quickly located A-gamer—a white, mid-thirties, skinny man wearing baggy jeans and an oversized tank top. A-gamer leaned over a pool table. His crew sat in chairs around the wall swigging beer. Mean streaks and dull wits crossed each of their brows.

A-gamer ignored Max's approach, but he did check out Joy. With confidence and force, he struck the cue ball.

Max reached out and stopped the ball before it hit its target.

A-gamer stood tall, holding the pool cue like a staff that could become a fighting stick at a moment's notice.

Max sized him up. He clearly wanted nothing more than to be king of grunge. His chosen grunge-wear included a tattoo on his neck that said "HATE is GR8." Despite the message, the rhyme made it sound like a license plate slogan. Other sayings and messages spilled down his alabaster shoulders and arms. He had the standard chain on his wallet—probably needed it in this bar—and a thick gold chain with an upside-down cross around his neck. Top that with a backwards baseball cap over buzzed hair, and Max couldn't resist a barb. "Eminem—you haven't changed a bit." A-gamer's crew, a punk group of half a dozen, held their collective breath.

A-gamer laughed. "And you got that funky-ass buzz cut, trying to be the rebel you're not. I know who I am. And you're a cop with a bad haircut."

"Ouch," said Max. He turned to Joy. "I totally deserved that."

Joy smiled. "Yes, you did." She turned to A-gamer. "Nice salvo. Now I know how you got your name."

Max suspected that Joy's flattery was a ruse. He saw the way

A-gamer's eyes roved over Joy's body. She played him, and he responded.

"That's right," said A-gamer. "I'm on my game at all times."

Joy said, "We'll let you get back to it. We just have a couple of questions."

Max jumped in. "You loaned money to Anne Martin."

A-gamer tensed. "On my game here too. You're not pinning her murder on me. I had nothin' to do with it. I was here with my boys."

"But you did give her a loan?" asked Max.

A-gamer kept his mouth shut.

Joy tried. "If we can't clear you, then we have to take you in for questioning. So help us out here."

"Yeah, I helped her out," said A-gamer. "I'm generous like that."

Max added, "And you upped the interest so she couldn't pay it back."

"She paid me back—go ask your chief. I'm pretty sure he bankrolled her and banged her," sniped A-gamer. "I'd be happy to testify against him."

Joy ignored his comment. "She paid you in cash?"

"Or other goods?" asked Max, giving A-gamer some latitude.

A lascivious grin crossed A-gamer's face. "Blondie—she'd do anything it took to keep her account current." A-gamer used caution in choosing his words. He eyed Joy and smirked.

"But not sex." Max turned to Joy. "She'd never sink *that* low." Max had to wonder if that was true, given that Anne had slept with Eugene to get what she needed.

A-gamer sniped back, "Like I wanted that Marilyn Monroe phony? I didn't want your chief's seconds."

Max's blood boiled. He had gotten to know Anne, a troubled girl with a kind heart who proved to be her own worst enemy. She'd hit bottom. Grant had cut her off, so had the casino. She made stupid mistakes. Maybe she even used men, but she didn't deserve a creep like A-gamer squeezing her along with everyone else.

In one swift move, Max grabbed A-gamer's cue stick, shoved him up against the wall, and pressed the stick against his skinny throat. "Anne Martin—that was her name. She was a nurse. She helped people. And you didn't help her. Like everyone else—you used her. I think you killed her to shut her up about your loan business, because she brought the chief of police to your door."

Joy neither smiled nor frowned. She tilted her head, like examining a specimen under a microscope—Max.

A-gamer grinned at having riled the cop. "Looks like he's playin' bad cop and you're playin' good cop." A-gamer leered at Joy. "If you play bad cop, I'll let you handle my cue stick."

At this, A-gamer's crew laughed.

"Thanks for the invite," said Joy, "but it looks to me like you're happier playing with your stick all by yourself."

Max asked, "Did Anne bring you drugs from the hospital?"

"You're not my type—so back off!" A-gamer's face contorted in fiery dismissal.

Max shot back. "You're my type A-gamer. The type I love to put behind bars. Until I know who killed Anne Martin, you'll be seeing a lot of me. So don't leave town." Max tossed the cue on the table, spun around, and marched toward the door. Joy followed.

At the door, Max said, "Nice salvo."

"You too." Joy pushed the door open and stepped into the daylight. "He's kinda right about your hair. It's not you."

Max rubbed his buzzed temples. "I know. I did it strictly to piss off dad and assert my independence. I didn't fully comprehend that until he passed away. I hated it the day I got it, but it's growing out."

Joy threw on her sunglasses. "I shaved my head just before I started high school. I was over trying to make friends. I think demon training begins in middle school."

"Did your dad give you crap for it?"

"A former FBI profiler? Not even close. He knew exactly why I'd done it. So he did the worst thing possible."

Max grinned, "He said he liked it."

"Yep, said I had a well-shaped head, so it looked good. I let it grow out starting that day. Rebelling against someone with stellar skills in criminal psychology wasn't easy." Joy opened the car door and slid in the passenger seat.

Max turned the key in the ignition. "I know that feeling. Dad would say he knew what I was thinking before I did—and he wasn't kidding. I know a great spot for iced tea, and we can go over the case at the same time."

"Iced tea sounds good. I'm parched." Joy buckled up.

Max drove to the valley's first vineyard, the Raedwald Wolf Estate Winery, at the end of Via Vendage. He parked before a sprawling modern-day Scottish castle and hopped out.

Max and Joy strolled through a beige stone archway and into a massive square with signs pointing to the restaurant, tasting rooms, and a quaint three-story hotel.

As soon as Max entered the restaurant, a woman with naturally curly, long, red hair rushed forward. She threw her arms around Max and squeezed him with deep affection. "Max! Good to see you. Who's your friend?" She had a Scottish brogue.

"Kate, this is Dr. Joy Burton. Joy, this is Kate, one of the owners of the winery and a chef and my godmother."

Joy began to put out a hand to shake, but Kate rushed in with a hug. "Sorry, love, but if you're with this boy, you're family. Come. Red will want to see you."

Kate led them back across the courtyard to the tasting room, where Max received the same reaction from a burly man with thick red-blond hair and a full beard. "Max!" He gave Max a bear hug, before extending a hand to Joy. "I'm Red."

A red-haired, freckle-faced, clean-shaven man behind the counter, about thirty and clearly Red and Kate's son, waved. "Hey, Max."

Max waved back. "Hi, Alfie."

Joy shook Red's hand.

"'Tis a joy, indeed," quipped Red. "I'm sure you've heard that one before."

Joy couldn't help but laugh. "A time or two."

"Come on—I'll get you some iced teas. I assume you're on duty," said Red with a Scottish lilt.

"We are. Can we sit out back? We have some noodling to do, and I couldn't think of a nicer place to noodle," said Max.

Kate gushed, "That's because there isn't a nicer place. How have you been, Max? Doin' okay?" Her voice held genuine concern.

"Getting there, Kate. Thanks for helping with the funeral arrangements. I—"

"No explanations needed." Red waved his hand. "We miss David too. We'll get you a table and send over some snacks. You've got to come over for dinner one night, though. Joy, that includes you."

The way Kate gushed, Max jumped in before the Wolf's got the wrong idea. "Hey guys, slow down. For one, Joy is my teacher. And for two, we're working together right now."

"The offer still stands for dinner," said Kate. "How about it?"

Joy said, "I'd love to. Thank you."

Kate sucked in a breath as an idea flooded her mind. "Red, how about Friday night? It's Lizzy's birthday party. And Sally can be such a handful. How about two more?" She turned to Max and Joy. "Sometimes, I want to kill that woman. I've never met a woman so rude, but she's Lizzy's sister, so we have to invite her."

Red put an arm around Kate as if to ring in the vitriol before a new guest. "Sally is Sally. She likes to shock people, get 'em riled is all. I'll seat her on my end of the table, Kate."

Kate's fiery red hair matched the fire in her words. "Well, you better. Because the last time she sat by me, I wanted to take the knight's lance and run her through." Kate turned back to her guests. "Lizzy would love to see you. So will her boys, Max."

"Now that be true." Red squeezed Kate again, this time in genuine affection. "Come. The both of ye."

Joy lit up. "I'd love to, if...Max?"

"Sure. What time?" asked Max.

"Six for cocktails. We'll watch the sun set and then go in for dinner," said Kate. "And since you two aren't an item—bring dates if you'd like."

Red and Kate led Max and Joy to a table on the terrace and disappeared. Beyond the balustrade railing, the vineyard stretched out as far as the eyes could see. Rows of stalks, thick with plump, ripe grape clusters, awaited the September harvest.

Max filled Joy in on his history with the Wolf family. "Raedwald and Katherine, Red and Kate for short, are...or were...Dad's best friends. They've spoiled me rotten since I was knee-high. They're my godparents. 'Red' was the last child born in his family. His parents didn't plan to have another child."

"The oops," said Joy.

"Yep. They doted on Red, spoiled him since *he* was knee-high. But the eldest brother inherited the titles and Scottish manor house. Red and his other siblings inherited a bundle of money though. Red and Kate, barely out of college, came to America. Red said he'd build his own castle, and here it is. He was the first in the valley to plant grapes. That was in 1972. Whatever you do, don't get him started on Scottish history or the peerage, like the differences between dukes and earls, viscounts and barons, or you're in for a long story—about three glasses of Burgundy worth. The history of the Wolf name will lead to Viking raids in Scotland and elsewhere—that's about two glasses worth and more exciting than the peerage. The Wolfs make an award-winning Pinot Noir too, so on the other hand, it's well worth it."

Joy laughed. "No doubt, you made that mistake."

"I did, but I don't regret it. This is one of the nicest families in Wine Valley. Red and Kate had five sons, but Danny died a month ago, pancreatic cancer. They have two daughters-in-law and a few red-haired grandchildren."

"Did you know that red-haired people don't go gray? Instead, their hair fades from copper to strawberry-blond to white. Forensic trivia."

A waitress dropped off two large iced teas and a cheese plate with crackers, bread slices, grapes, nuts and dried fruits.

"So who's at the top of your list?" Joy cut a wedge of white cheddar, stuck it on an apple wedge, topped it with a walnut, and popped it in her mouth.

Max dove for the brie and bread. "Dr. Grant, for one. He wanted to walk Anne home after the game, but she refused. Maybe he hung around and saw her double back to party with Eugene. He left, got drunk, and came back. He might have tried to confront her and lost control. His knuckles looked bruised but that's not concrete evidence."

"A-gamer is no saint. Maybe he wanted to kill Anne to set an example to others. Or she refused to be his pipeline to the hospital. She brought Goldsby in. That might have sealed her fate. A-gamer has good reason to frame the chief," said Joy. "Maybe Shane was a source too. The hospital noticed drug diversion. Maybe Shane worried the pharmacy was on to him, so he tried to sever ties with A-gamer. Or Deon."

Max agreed, "Could be. A lot of them had access to drugs. I'll have Captain Banks put surveillance on A-gamer."

"And we only know Eugene's side of the story. A night of passion." Joy popped a grape in her mouth. "For all we know, he felt used, followed her home, and struck the blow. Then drowned her to keep her quiet. Shane's death may be unrelated. Or maybe—and this is creepy—daddy wants Cynthia all to himself."

Max ate Brie with a couple of walnuts. "Maybe. But I still like Grant. He's a loose cannon. And a doctor would know exactly how much to overdose a guy Shane's size. But that presumes Grant had motive to kill Shane. We've got no connection. And Shane used drugs. He may not have realized he ODed."

Joy sipped her tea. "I don't know Goldsby as well as you do. He's still on my radar. He had motive for wanting Anne dead, since he'd helped her solve the A-gamer problem. And Anne told Shane. If it got back to Goldsby, it gives him motive. He'd lose his everything he'd worked for."

Max said, "I'll tail Grant tonight. The income he's been making with Kinsey Pharmaceuticals is good, but not enough to support his lifestyle. He's got to be supplementing his income."

Joy corrected Max. "*We* will tail Grant, partner."

"I'll pick you up at five?"

Joy smiled, "It's a date." She corrected herself, "Not a date-date. I'll be wearing black and accessorizing with a Glock."

"I've no doubt," said Max.

"Technically, to scientists, black isn't a color at all. Light rays contain a spectrum of color. Black is the void. The absence of all color." Joy sat back and stared out over the hills etched with rows of leafy grape stalks. "You're lucky, Max. I didn't have godparents or someone like Belle to act as a surrogate grandmother. It was just me and Sam—an FBI profiler who wrote books on true crime and serial killers. Your life is full of color."

"I would agree with that." Max popped the last of the Brie into his mouth. "And full of delicious food."

14

Max picked up Joy as planned. To his surprise, she lived in a sprawling single-level ranch-styled home that sat atop a hill on a sprawling tract of land, demarcated by white fences. The street was a long row of custom-built ranch houses, each set back from the road like grand country estates.

Max drove his father's black Ford F-150 with a super-cab that, despite the moniker "super cab," had just enough room for two, or a third person squeezed in real tight, and the back seat would only fit small people, not men with full-grown legs.

Joy hopped in. She wore black leggings and a black long-sleeved shirt She dropped a backpack at her feet.

"Nice house," said Max.

"Dad bought it for cheap before the boom. I didn't know he owned it. I thought it belonged to a friend who traveled a lot, and we just borrowed it when we came here on vacation. But the deed was in a box with his papers."

Max wound down the hill toward the gate. "I grew up in an old house. I mean old. Dad bought a run-down, boarded-up hacienda built in the 1920s by Juan de Flores, known as Don Juan, one of the first ranchers in the valley. He situated the house so that it overlooked Hawk Valley, where his cattle roamed. Today, housing developments surround the property. But it's been home for as long I can remember. Dad was a do-it-yourselfer. He liked taking that old house and giving it a new life. After dad died, I gave up my apartment in town and moved back to the hacienda."

Max left it there. He didn't add the reason why: the old beams caressed him like the trunk of a strong tree; its branches protected him; its roots dug so deep that no twister nor tempest could uproot him. The house, which his dad simply called "The Ranch" kept him grounded as he found his way in this terrifying new world devoid of his father.

"Sounds beautiful."

"It is." Max drove out the gate and down the road. "Um, you are aware that you dressed like a robber?" Max wore black tactical pants and a black police-issue polo shirt. Two body armor vests with yellow lettering that spelled out POLICE sat on the seat between them.

Joy mused, "Nah, for burglary, I wear gloves and a beanie."

"Not in August. Then you'd really stand out as a robber," said Max.

"Good point." Joy looked around. "Nice truck."

"It's Dad's. Baby Blue is too conspicuous for a stake out."

"Baby Blue? Oh my God, you named your car?"

Max turned onto Via Vendage, heading away from the wineries and up into the hills. "Baby blue Mustang convertible with latte-colored leather interior. Bought her used, but she's a classic beauty."

Joy remarked, "You're right. Conspicuous."

"What do you drive?"

"I kept Dad's Chevy Tahoe. Black."

"Naturally."

"Sam painted the entire Wine Valley house sunshine yellow. He also liked daisies."

"Daisies? Now that you mention it, my dad seemed to like them too. There's a daisy painting on the wall in the living room—overshadowed by the red and yellow plaid furniture. David King loved plaid. "

"Ouch. That trumps yellow."

"Yep."

Max found a spot to park above the gated entrance to Dr. Grant's estate. If the doctor pulled in or out, Max and Joy would see him. They didn't have to wait long. Grant pulled in at half-past five and out at seven thirty. The sun had nearly set, but twilight lingered as Dr. Grant's red Porsche Boxster sped down the hill.

"Now that's conspicuous," said Joy. "I wonder what he named her? Lady in Red? Foxy Lady?"

Max played along. "Hot Lips."

By the time Dr. Grant pulled into the parking lot of Eugene's mortuary, Max and Joy had exhausted good names and drifted to the sillier ones like "Candy, as in candy apple" and the more obvious, like "Cherry."

Max turned off his headlights and rolled to a stop on the gravel.

Grant stepped out of the car and walked around the side of the building.

Max grabbed his police vest and handed the other to Joy. "Let's give them a few minutes to get comfortable."

Joy reached into her backpack and pulled out a Glock 17.

Max jumped out of the truck and lifted his Glock 19 from his hip holster. He pulled the slide and dropped a bullet into the chamber. Cops always carried their weapons loaded and with a bullet in the chamber. Big town or quaint valley town—it didn't matter.

Max led the way, edging along the side of the building, following Grant's trail. A full moon cast unwanted silvery light.

At the back of the building, light radiated from two windows on either side of a steel door, but the windows sat too high up to peek through. Max could hear classical music and a buzzing sound. He signaled to Joy that he would enter first, and she was to follow.

Joy gave him an affirmative hand signal.

Max turned the handle. The door was unlocked. The moment it cracked open, the music grew louder. Max flung the door open, rushed inside, and pointed his gun. "Freeze!"

Joy fell in behind Max, gun aimed, finger on the trigger guard.

Cynthia yelped and threw her hands in the air. She stood beside what looked like a meat locker.

Eugene and Grant froze in place.

A body lay on a metal embalming table in a room that was too white and pure, as if the surgical procedure under way needed to be sterile. Hoses suspended overhead, steel counters lined with ghoulish instruments, and a large white freezer gave the room the appearance of Frankenstein's laboratory.

Max and Joy faced a grisly sight—Dr. Grant, wearing a heavy apron and goggles, held a small, electric, circular saw in his hand. He had severed the legs and arms from the body, like cutting up a chicken, leaving raw ends of flesh, bone, and severed arteries exposed. The corpse, nothing but a torso with a head, could not protest the ghastly dissection. Grant had only to sever the head when stopped by the intruders.

Eugene had been wrapping an arm in plastic when stopped. "Put down those weapons. There's nothing illegal going on here!"

Max's brain could not comprehend the words "nothing illegal," except that neither the doctor, nor Eugene, nor Cynthia seemed rattled.

Dr. Grant laughed and set down his saw. The moment he released the trigger, the saw whined to a stop. "You followed me. I'm touched. Eugene, turn the music down, will you?"

Neither Max nor Joy would drop their weapons, so Eugene said, "I'm just reaching for the volume control. Don't shoot. There's a brochure behind you. Pick it up and read it."

Joy picked one up and read it aloud while Max kept his gun on the group. "The Grant and Carter Institute for Biomedical Donations. Donate your body to science." Joy eyed Grant and Eugene then continued reading:

- *Eliminate expensive funeral costs: free transport and cremation*
- *Your generous gift of tissue will contribute to scientific study*
- *Next of kin can approve this gift for the deceased*
- *The only restrictions are no infectious diseases (testing is free); no severe obesity*
- *Surgical implants and scars are acceptable; no age restrictions*
- *Cremated remains, upon request, will be returned to the family within weeks*

"You guys are body brokers." Joy said it like an accusation. She lowered her Glock. "Put down the gun, Max. This will spoil your appetite and curl your hair, but he's right. It's not illegal."

Max holstered his weapon. "What's a body broker?"

Cynthia lowered her hands.

Dr. Grant and Eugene grinned as Joy explained, "Organ donation is strictly regulated in the US, like when you check the box to donate your organs at the DMV and you get the little pink dot on your driver's license, but 'tissue' donation is not as strictly regulated—these guys use the word 'tissue' because they wouldn't get any takers if they said, 'donate your loved one's arms, legs, head, and torso to science,.' Families believe they are doing a wonderful thing—"

"They are," defended Eugene. "Medical schools around the country need real bodies to teach medical students."

Grant added. "Right. We are not 'body brokers.' We are a 'non-transplant tissue bank.'"

Joy pointed her Glock at them. "Interrupt me again, and I'll have to shoot you on the grounds of rudeness alone."

Eugene huffed and crossed his arms. Cynthia closed the freezer lid, and Grant shut his mouth.

Max liked Joy's spunk. He could imagine her pulling the trigger, Grant falling down dead, and Joy walking away, saying, "I warned him not to speak, didn't I?"

Joy continued. "It's a perfect match, Max. Lots of funeral directors push these donations for a finder's fee. The dead person doesn't have to approve it—the next of kin can sign. In this case, these guys aren't the middle men—they *are* the brokers. They pocket a fortune from selling body parts. And there isn't a lot of regulation about who can start such a company—you don't even have to have a doctor cut up the body—and there isn't much regulation as to who can buy the parts either. They're even shipped overseas. A whole chicken is cheaper than its parts—same for car, and same for a body. A whole cadaver might go anywhere from three to five grand— depending on market supply, but a torso with legs might sell for close to four grand, skin ten dollars per square inch, bones and ligaments packaged separately. Prices go up when supplies go down and vice versa. What's a head cost these days?"

"A pretty penny," said Grant. "These parts help companies create new medical devices. A company might need elbows to test a new joint or to train doctors to install them properly."

Eugene smirked, "We even rent pieces. They can be returned and sold again."

Max winced, "Rented? That's disgusting!"

Grant shot back, "Look, this may not be pretty to you, but I trained on cadavers."

"I get that," said Max. "But I agree with Joy. Nothing in your brochure lets families know that their 'generous tissue donation' is putting money in your pockets and sending their loved one's pieces to hell and back."

Grant fired up the saw. "If you'll excuse me, I've got to get back to work. You're welcome to stick around and watch."

Max had seen enough. He stormed out.

Joy jumped in the truck. Max stomped on the gas and the tires spun in the gravel before getting traction.

By the time Max pulled up to Joy's house, they'd barely said two words. Max put the truck in park and rubbed his eyes. "Back to square one. See you tomorrow."

"Don't take this the wrong way—like a date or anything— 'cause it's not—but I'm not leaving you like this. Come in. I'll pour us a drink."

"Another time."

In one deft movement, Joy turned off the engine, yanked the key out of the ignition, opened the door, hopped to the ground, grabbed her backpack, and ran up to the front door. "You can sit there until the sun comes up—or you can have one stinking drink! Your choice!" She spun on the heels of her black combat boots, marched toward the front door, unlocked it, and disappeared.

15

Max no longer liked Joy's spunk. He jumped out, determined to beat her at her own game. She'd hand him a drink. He'd down it in a single shot, get his keys back, and head home where he'd pour another drink and sip it while his brain rehashed the evidence and suspects.

Max stepped inside, comforted by the warmth. The foyer light lit up a distressed white table and filtered into a dining room with botanical green prints and the same distressed white furniture, like a French cafe in the country.

Max let out a guilty breath. Why was he blaming Joy for his disappointment at not solving the case and rudely retreating? She was his partner. He needed to act like it.

A flickering glow, like from a gas fireplace, emanated from the living room up ahead. He strolled in that direction, past yellow walls and under white ceilings.

Max reached the living room and plunked down on a canary yellow sofa that sprouted red and white irises on green leafy stalks. It was like falling into a patch of wildflowers. He sat opposite an elegant stone fireplace surrounded by built-in cabinets with under-cabinet lights, one of which illuminated a framed photo and a bottle of whiskey.

Max tilted his head back and closed his eyes. "I'm here, Joy. And I'm not moving another inch!"

The warmth relaxed Max. He worked to get the grisly scene at the mortuary out of his head. He thought of his walk beside Goldfish Creek. Then his thoughts drifted to Joy. Despite her being pretty, witty and smart, not to mention her ability to handle a Glock, Max never mixed business with pleasure. He hoped she didn't either.

"Max," Joy said in the same don't-get-excited voice she'd used on the chief and A-gamer. "Don't move, okay? Keep your eyes closed."

Oh, crap! Did he misread women or what? Max opened his mouth to speak and opened his eyes at the same time. In his peripheral vision to his right, something flicked at him. He turned his head and came face-to-face with the head of a snake —a huge head. It flicked its pink forked tongue.

Max froze. His eyes popped wide open. He was so close, he saw the snake's golden scales and the crisp black stripe that ran from nostrils to cheek and its bulging, glossy, black eyes. It had a flat, black-topped head and a white underside.

Max felt the strike of its pink tongue against his nose. If not for his training, he would have bolted to the ceiling by now and not come down anytime soon.

"Shhhh," said Joy as she nestled her legs up to the edge of the sofa between Max's legs. That sound. He knew that sound! That same calming, shushing sound from his youth. Max stared into Joy's face. His eyes cringed as she leaned over him.

Joy reached out, scooped up the snake from the back of the sofa, and stepped back. "Monty, bad girl. Sorry, Max. I should have named her Houdini. She is quite the escape artist." Joy had not changed clothes, but she had thrown on a red and black silk robe. She plunked down beside Max, pulled her legs up, and crossed them. She coiled Monty—who had to be five feet long—in her lap and covered her with the flap of her robe. Monty's head emerged and rested on Joy's slender belly. Joy stroked Monty's head. "I set your drink on the end table."

"All of a sudden, I could use one." Max sat up straight. He grabbed the glass and shot back the amber liquid, swallowing it in one gulp. It was whiskey. Good Scotch whiskey. It burned his throat in a pleasing way. "What is that?"

"Monty is a ball python. She just turned twenty-one. Come on, girl. Time for bed." Joy carried the snake down the hall. When Joy returned, she sat next to Max. "Sorry it's warm in here. Monty likes it that way. So do I."

It had been one hell of a day. The under-counter lights lit up the bottle of Scotch. It glowed like a beacon, drawing Max toward it. The warmth of the room relaxed his nerves, or maybe it was the Scotch. Frankly, he didn't care. Max grabbed his glass and crossed the room.

"Monty—python. Cute. My dad and I liked..." As Max poured himself another drink, his eyes caught hold of a silver frame. Two men, smiling like best friends, stood side-by-side holding fishing poles. Each of them held up a string of fish. He knew the picture well—he had one just like it at home.

Max grabbed the frame and spun around. "Is this some kind of twisted joke? Who are you?"

Joy set Max's keys on the distressed white coffee table. "I hoped you could tell me, Max." Joy tossed back her drink and held out her empty glass. "Refill, please."

Max stuffed the bottle under his arm and returned to the sofa. He set his glass down on the table and set the picture between them. He refilled Joy's glass. "Why do you have this picture of my father?"

Joy bolted forward, unable to contain her excitement. She

sat on the edge of the sofa. "I knew it! You have the same picture, don't you? It's a picture of my father, Sam Burton. I've thought about this moment for a long while now. Dad died in January, shot by a sniper. I was there when it happened. I've wasted so much time, Max. I dove into an abyss of depression. But when I came out, I found keys to a storage unit. Clues led me here, like the photo."

Joy snatched the picture from the sofa and struggled with the clips on the back. "Dad had this in a white wooden frame. I bought this silver frame for it. When I went to change it out, I saw this." She pulled the back off of the frame and handed the picture to Max.

Max stared at the image. He flipped it over. A note on the back read, "Find Pride."

Joy elaborated, "Pride. Something clicked. I found the deed to this house. A few weeks back, I came here to look for answers. My dad and I ate at Belle's when we came to town for vacations. I went there and asked Belle if she knew the other man in the picture. She did. David King. I was so excited! All I had to do was find him, and I'd have answers. Then she told me he'd just passed, and that it was his funeral that day. I went. I saw you. I recognized you, but you didn't recognize me."

It was time to ask his question. "Did you have a kitten? One that died?"

Joy's chin bobbed up and down. "I think I found it and wanted to help it. I don't think it was mine...like a pet. I don't know."

Max's mind exploded like a picture made of glass. The shards flew off in all directions: Anne's dead body in the lake, body parts being severed and wrapped, Joy's lecture about evidence, A-gamer holding the pool cue, Monty flicking her tongue, and now, a little dark-haired girl holding a dead kitten, who grew up before his eyes into Joy.

Max had wanted answers, but knowing he'd found his

childhood companion, the dark-haired girl with the kitten, suddenly overwhelmed him. His life had already been turned upside down in so many ways—he couldn't handle another flip.

Max tossed back his drink, grabbed his keys, and shot out of the house. He heard, "Max! Wait!" but he didn't wait.

Max jumped into his truck, revved the engine, and spun the wheels until traction propelled him down the driveway to the gate. He rested his head against his hands, which gripped the steering wheel like his life depended on it.

He lifted his head and hit the gas pedal, barely waiting for the gate to swing wide enough to let his truck pass through. He shot forward into the road and veered hard right.

A horn blared. The street had minimal lights and hardly any traffic, but he'd cut off a car that had the bad luck to be in his way at the wrong time.

Every street along his route home felt like a labyrinth in a place he'd never known before. The darkness closed in on him, threatening to change everything he knew to be the truth into a lie.

When Max reached his turnoff, he stomped on the gas and shot toward the house. He raced around the curved driveway that encircled an old oak tree and braked hard. The truck lurched to a stop.

Max leaped out and rushed to get inside, like he needed sanctuary, a familiar haven.

In his mind's eye, he saw an explosion. *Boom!* His cheeks flushed with heat. His heart raced. His life exploded. It was a memory, boiling up from the deep. But a memory of what? And when?

Max fumbled with his keys. It all hit him faster than he could comprehend. He remembered his father's last words in the ambulance as he died: "Pride and joy. Find...Joy." He thought he meant happiness. What the hell was going on?

Max shoved the door open, flipped on the lights, and

grabbed the framed picture sitting on the mantle over the fire-place. He ripped the back off and read the words. "Find Joy." Joy was capitalized.

Max hung his head. He'd lost his father. Joy had lost hers too. Where would they get answers now?

He'd already grieved for his father's death, but now anger welled within him. Why? Why did these two men keep secrets? One thing Max knew for sure: David King had loved Max every day to the day he died. David had tried so hard to speak to him in the ambulance, but Max wouldn't let him. David had ripped off his oxygen mask and pleaded with him, "Max, you gotta know."

But Max shushed him.

David King ran out of time.

Max grabbed his phone. It didn't even ring a full time before Joy picked up. "Max! Are you okay?"

"I'm sorry."

"No, I'm sorry. I should have waited. I sprang it on you."

"I wanted to ask you about the kitten at the funeral," confessed Max.

"We'll figure this out. I was so stupid, Max." Joy let out an audible whimper. "This is all my fault. Sam died months ago! Months! But I...I wallowed in this pit of depression. Had I started going through Sam's things earlier...but I didn't. I didn't figure it out, until it was too late."

"You found me."

"But your dad had the answers."

Max felt a sudden calm, born of resolution not of conviction —they could only go forward. Who had named them Pride and Joy? How did they end up in the hands of two law enforcement officers, two single men who adopted them? And why did those men, clearly friends, keep them apart?

"Max, are you there?"

"Yeah. I was just thinking that it's a good thing I'm a detective and you were raised by an FBI profiler. We'll find the answers."

"Damn straight we will, Max."

"See you tomorrow, pardner."

Joy let out an audible laugh mixed with a release of guilty torment. "Sleep well—no homework."

Max hung up the phone.

As he hovered beneath the hot shower and let the water pound his head and back, the obvious answers came first—they'd both been adopted, so clearly, they'd lived in the same foster home. Given their opposite appearances, Max leaned toward that hypothesis. Twins looked alike, even if fraternal and one was a boy and the other a girl. Joy was dark. He was fair. He ran off of instinct; she ran off of calculations. She had dark eyes; his were blue. She was a genius; he was no dummy but not a genius.

Max dried off and pulled on pajama bottoms. He jumped beneath the covers. His brain kept asking questions, but the alcohol and sheer tiredness caused them to fade.

In his sleep, fitful nightmares punctuated with the happiest memories of his life flashed through his mind. The peace and bliss brought on by happy memories didn't last, like riding a pony at the Wild West Harvest Festival with David King jogging along beside him.

Those happy moments shattered into glassy shards and flew away. Were they even real? He tried to grab the pieces and put them back together.

The razor sharp edges slashed his palms.

Blood oozed onto the mosaic he'd spent the night assembling and reassembling.

Right before he woke up, he'd almost succeeded, but the picture he'd pieced together showed a portrait of one face compiled from many: his blue right eye, Joy's brown left eye, his father's nose, Sam Burton's cheek, his blond hair framing half of the face, her black hair framing the other. And a couple of pieces he didn't recognize.

Max shot awake and bolted upright, sweating, quaking, seething.

16

By the time Max reached the station, he'd didn't know what to say to Joy. Suddenly, he didn't like change, and Joy could change everything. David King must have had good reasons to keep him apart from Joy—so why dig up the past? So what if David King wasn't his birth father. He knew that. But he also knew David King was his father. A damn good one.

David had taught him well, like to focus on his job. Max found Joy at her desk. His tone was all business. "Back to square one. Let's see how Eugene and Cynthia react to finding out Shane is dead."

Joy set down her half-full mug of coffee and jumped to her feet, clearly caught off guard by Max's demeanor, but she recovered quickly. "Good idea. I'd like to observe their natural habitat too. That might give me a clue to understanding them better."

From the moment Max drove his unmarked car out of the parking structure, he kept his lips sealed.

Joy fidgeted, let out a couple of heavy sighs, and mumbled under her breath.

Max knew she wanted to talk, but he didn't. He kept his eyes on the road and his lips sealed tight.

Finally, Joy blurted, "We have to talk about this, Max."

"Nope," he said. "We don't. I changed my mind. I don't want to know."

"Alright, I respect that, but I do, so..." Joy reached down and pulled a box out of her backpack. "All I need from you is a sample, and I'll leave you out of it."

"A sample? What is that?"

"It's a sibling DNA test kit. This will show if we're brother and sister or complete strangers."

"Are you serious? Look at us. Forget it. You can try to unseal your adoption papers."

"That will take months of legal wrangling with the state of California. And a judge could still refuse to unseal them. Both of our fathers are dead—it would have been helpful if they had signed off on it. I already looked into this. If I had some genetic disease—cancer, for example—a judge might say yes for medical reasons, but the 'I just want to know who my real parents are angle doesn't work. I even searched FBI records while I was employed there. Nothing. Just the adoption birth certificates. Max, all I need is a thimble full of spit, literally, and in three to five days, we'll know. I'll know."

Max surveyed the hills on either side of him. He had a new appreciation for them—they remained the same. Immutable. Even if charred or burned, they would recover and be there, year after year, long after he left the Earth. The only changes in them amounted to seasonal color: now gold and brown with spots of olive-green, but lush green by January after the winter rains, then covered in vibrant splotches of purple and orange and yellow in late February or early March when the wild-flowers bloomed, then gold again when the summer heat withered them bone dry.

Max turned off the main road and onto a two-lane road that led to Eugene's house.

"Just think about it," said Joy. "That's all I'm asking. If you don't want to know, I won't share the results. Max, look at me."

Max pulled into the clearing before Eugene's house and parked the car. He peered into her dark pleading eyes.

"I...I need to know." Joy's voice trembled. "You feel fixed, secure. I never have. I've never felt like I belonged. I didn't have any friends growing up—except for Monty. And I didn't just shave my head." Joy peeled back the long sleeve of her white cotton shirt. She showed Max a faint scar on her right wrist, a hesitation mark at best.

"That's a scratch, not a scar."

"That's because I realized I was insane for even thinking about it! Hamlet ruined it for me."

"Excuse me? Hamlet? Maybe you are insane."

"Actually, I'm pretty smart. So I figured it out—'to be or not to be.' Hamlet hates his life. His uncle poisoned his father and married his mother. So he's thinking of suicide, of taking his 'bare bodkin,' a knife, and killing himself, so he can 'sleep,' die, but then he starts to think—wait—if I'm dead, I'll dream, and if I dream, maybe I'll have nightmares, and maybe the living nightmare is better than the one I'll have if I kill myself. And then he realizes he thought about it too much, so now he can't possibly go through with it, because thinking has 'made him a coward.'"

Max stared long and hard. "Was that supposed to make sense?"

Joy said, "Bottom line, Max. It's not always the deepest cuts that hurt the most."

"No wonder you dove into psychology and sociology. You're overthinking this. Obsessed. Let it go, Hamlet."

"I'm not obsessed. I just want what you have. Give me a chance to get grounded."

Max paused. He grabbed the wheel to hold on to something that could anchor him. He curled his fingers around it and squeezed until his knuckles turned white. He needed to feel something solid. "What if grounding you shatters me? Did you think about that?"

"I won't let that happen."

"You can't make that promise!"

Max jumped out of the vehicle, slammed the car door, and stomped to Eugene's front door.

As Joy caught up to him, Max knocked. When he had spotted Joy on the hill at the funeral, he felt that inner pang to dig. But now, realizing all that he might unearth, he threw down the shovel. Some part of him knew something of the past. A gut feeling. It wasn't pretty. And that young part of him, that little boy, had dug a pit, put the past in it, and heaped on the dirt. He'd buried it so deep, he couldn't remember it. There had to be a good reason for that.

Cynthia swung the door open. She wore her usual apron over a denim dress. "Detective King."

"Hi, Cynthia. I'm sorry if I scared you last night at the mortuary. Just doing my job. This is Dr. Joy Burton. She's working with me now. Can we talk to you and your father for a minute? It's important."

"Sure. Come in. I just made a fresh coffee cake with cinnamon topping and icing swirls. It's papa's favorite. Made from scratch. I'll get you a piece."

"That sounds lovely, Cynthia. Thank you," said Joy, already following her inside.

"Coffee or tea?" asked Cynthia, delighted by Joy's quick acceptance.

"Green tea if you have it," said Joy. "Black if you don't."

"I do. And for you, Detective King?"

"Coffee, black." He really did look forward to fresh coffee cake topped with sugar. He used sugar like salve, and this morning, he needed lots of salve. His dad used to cook waffles or buckwheat pancakes on the weekends, or sometimes, they stopped at the local donut shop. That was why he liked donuts so much—they came with family ties.

Eugene had been reading a book when they came in. His face formed a scowl upon seeing them. "Here to arrest me?"

Max and Joy sat in the floral chairs opposite the sofa.

Max apologized, even though he hadn't done anything wrong. He needed to diffuse a hostile witness. David King would say, "Give 'em sugar and butter 'em up until they slide right through your palms and land in the roasting pan, right where you want 'em." "Mr. Carter, I do apologize for breaking in on you. It may not make you feel any better, but we were tailing Dr. Grant. Not you. We have to follow all leads. I hope you understand."

Cynthia brought over pieces of cake on floral china plates and handed them out. She took Eugene's empty cup away to refill it. "That's what I told, Papa. You have a job to do, and you need to do it." Cynthia brought Joy her tea, Max his coffee, and rushed back to the kitchen.

Joy dug her fork into the cake and ate a bite. "Wow! I'm not much of a cook, Cynthia. This is fabulous!"

Max wished he'd said it first. Apparently, Joy knew about using sugar too—of course she did. It was her career in forensic psychology. Max took a bite. "Oh, man. You weren't kidding. Delicious."

"Well, there's plenty more," said Cynthia, beaming. She set down Eugene's refilled cup and a tea for herself and settled on the sofa.

Eugene snarled. He hadn't touched his cake yet. "I know you're not here for cake. Why are you here?"

Max set down his plate, as this was not the kind of news a person broke at a tea party. He leaned forward, rested his hands on his knees, and hung his head to show empathy. He swallowed the bite in his mouth. "I'm sorry, but Shane Drake is dead."

Cynthia set down her plate and sank into the crook of her father's arm. "Oh, Papa!"

Eugene wrapped protective arms around his daughter. "I'm stunned. What happened?"

Joy leaned forward. She set down her plate. "It looks like an overdose. I'm so sorry." Joy rose to her feet and paced the floor.

Max jumped in, "We're waiting for toxicology."

Cynthia let out muffled cries. "But Shane was always so careful with his medications."

Eugene rubbed Cynthia's back. "There, there, dear. We have each other." He addressed Max, "This is simply too much. Anne and Shane. Gone."

Cynthia mumbled, between gasps "I accepted...Shane's proposal. We were going...to live here with Papa."

Eugene said, "Shane told us he had an appointment to see a surgeon."

Joy peered inside the doll house. "Cynthia, this is a lovely doll house. Did your mother buy it for you?"

"No," said Cynthia. "Mother died years ago. Papa bought it for me."

Eugene gave Cynthia a squeeze. "Cynthia played with that house non-stop, unless she had homework."

Cynthia let out a nervous laugh. "Sometimes even when I did have homework, Papa. Remember the trip we made? When we found it?"

"Every time I see it," he said to Cynthia before elaborating. "We made a father-daughter trip to northern California one summer, and we found a delightful doll store and museum in Carmel. It hadn't been open that long. Magical place. Cynthia begged me to buy the house, and she's been furnishing it ever since."

Joy added, "Max, come see this."

"Please don't touch it," said Cynthia. "It's taken me years to get it just the way I like it."

Max finished his cake and set down the plate. He didn't have any interest in seeing a doll house, no matter how exquisite, but he humored Joy, figuring her request had a reason behind it.

When Max peered into the house, he had to admit he'd never seen anything like it. It had three stories, including an attic full of boxes and miniature trunks. One trunk was open. A framed photo lay face down on a folded quilt. The second floor had two bedrooms and two bathrooms. A man's green robe hung on the door in one bathroom, and a pink robe hung in the other. The first floor had a kitchen and living room. Floral furniture and burgeoning floral vases recreated the room in which Max stood. "Wow! Did you create the miniature house to match the big one, or the big one to match the miniature one?"

"That's an excellent question, Max," said Joy.

Eugene answered, "When we built this house, Cynthia used her doll house as a design. Of course this is single level, but we came close, didn't we, dear?"

"We did, Papa." In a new bout of tears, Cynthia added, "And Shane was going to share it with us."

Max and Joy returned to their seats. Max asked, "Did Shane have any business with Dr. Grant or Deon?"

Eugene responded, 'Not that I know of."

Cynthia wiped her eyes with her apron and whimpered.

Joy said, "We'll let you go."

Max and Joy showed themselves out.

Max slid into the driver's seat of his car and tensed with frustration. "We need connections."

Joy slid into the passenger seat. "Maybe it wasn't just Anne who knew A-gamer. Maybe Shane used his services too, and Anne found out."

Max fired up the engine. "Let's stop by Shane's pharmacy this afternoon."

17

R ather than heading back to the main road, Max turned off and drove down a less traveled dirt path. He rolled down his window to hear the creek, although he didn't need the sound for guidance.

As soon as he saw the flowing, brackish water, he parked beside three small trees that afforded some shade. Without a word, he jumped out of the vehicle, walked to the bank, and plunked down beneath a tree. He faced the creek and wondered if it had ever changed course—if in its history, some catastrophe, some drought or flood or earthquake had forced it to cut a new path.

Joy reached in the back seat and grabbed a well-worn red, white, and blue plaid blanket from the floorboard. She hopped out and headed toward Max. Joy spread out the blanket and sat down near him. "Want to share my blanket. You don't want to get your clothes dirty."

"That's the point, Joy. I hate to burst your bubble—not that you had hoped to be related to me—but I do get my clothes dirty. I'm a mess, you're tidy; I'm blonde, blue-eyed; you've got jet-back hair with brown eyes; I'm fairly intelligent; you're a freaking genius."

"Is your birthday November 14?" asked Joy.

"We don't even know if that's our real birthday—do we?"

"I remember an explosion."

Max tried to fight it off, but a memory bolted into his head.

"You remember it, too, don't you?" asked Joy.

Max struggled with all of his might to forget, to push the memory back into the grave, but memories didn't work like that. A familiar scent, an image, a voice, a memento, a song— and the memory splashes across a mega-sized movie screen, and the person cranking the old projector laughs because he's in charge, not you, and you're forced to watch. "I remember— or I think I remember an explosion."

"We were about three and a half," said Joy. "You cried."

"You didn't," said Max. "When I woke up, you were gone. Everything changed." Max shook his head. He didn't want to see any more, but the guy on the crank kept turning the handle. The projectionist let out a gut-deep laugh, as if to say "stay tuned, this is the good part." The camera angle—which coincided exactly with Max's gaze—panned upward, and he saw the face of the man who ran with him and shoved him inside the backseat of the car—David King. David's voice rang in his ears. "Hold on there, Pride and Joy. Ya hear? You're safe now."

And all of a sudden, a second face appeared. It came into focus for Max. The driver of the car turned to see the man in the back seat, and Max saw his profile—the man in the photo, holding the fish—Sam Burton.

Max hunched over. The heavy memories bent his head down like a weak tree pushed over in a tempest.

Max stared into Joy's dark eyes, but they were suddenly set in a child's face, and she sat beside him in the backseat of a dark car on a dark night. The car sped away from the hell-fire that devoured the house.

Joy said, "I remember a woman's face, maybe our foster

mother's. I think she was in the house when it exploded. I woke up in a princess-like bedroom, white and pink—I hate pink. Sam was there."

Max plucked at two golden stalks of grass and started tying them together. "Then she's dead. End of story."

"I wish," scoffed Joy. "You have Wine Valley. The perfect world. And perfect memories."

Max tossed the grass aside. "Was Sam a good father? Why do you call him Sam?"

"Sam could not have been a better father. But I call him Sam, because I never felt like I belonged to him. I didn't fit. I don't think I fit anywhere. I think I scared Sam. I scared myself growing up."

"Scared how?" asked Max.

"I'm fascinated with death." She let that hang in the air for a minute. "Like watching a bird eat a worm or a snake swallow a mouse."

Max remembered the way Joy had peered into Shane's face when they had found him dead. Sure, she studied it for discoloration and other clinical clues of his demise, but there was a spark of something else...fascination, allure, magnetism. He also sensed that Joy had protected him, kept him safe long ago. But safe from what? Or whom? It was a gut feeling. No memories supported the feeling.

Joy let her eyes follow the river. "You probably played with cowboy pistols growing up. I scouted the fields for dead things."

"Okay, I admit that's kinda weird, but I remember finding a flat lizard in the road in front of my house once, and I played with it for a while. Unless you killed them?" He held his breath, hoping for the right answer.

"No. But put me in a field like this one, and I'd find them. Dead insects, lizards, mice, birds. I'd poke them, turn them over, and get deeply lost in their dull fixed eyes. My real treasures, I'd take home, wrap them in a paper towel, and keep them in a shoebox under my bed. I had quite the collection of skeletons." Joy said it with clear pride.

Max suggested, "Maybe you wanted to help them, Joy. Like the kitten. Maybe you found it dead and wanted to bring it back to life or something. Heal it?"

"Dad said I just needed to make friends. So, when I was five, I took my shoebox to school to show the other kids. I actually thought they'd be as amazed as I was, and I'd be swimming with friends."

"Oh, man. For a smart girl, that was a totally dumb move," said Max.

Joy flopped onto her back and stared into the tree tops. "Hard lesson number one."

Max lay on one elbow, facing her. "What happened?"

Joy flipped onto her side to face Max. "I not only didn't make any friends after that—ever—I earned a few nicknames. It felt like every time I walked down the hallway or sidewalk from then on, those names flew at me like a hot branding iron. I did have one favorite though—Wednesday—you know, from the *Addams Family*. She was my hero—or anti-hero. She made me feel normal. I even decided 'screw the other kids,' and I dressed like Wednesday for Halloween. I'd watched the *Addams Family* movies a hundred times. I had Wednesday's hair: dark, long and parted in the middle."

Joy gushed with excitement. "You should have seen their faces when I strolled in with a deadpan face. I knew Wednesday's lines cold, like 'I'm a homicidal maniac. They look just like everyone else. The next year, I secretly snapped photos of the mean girls and stuck their faces on Girl Scout cookies using icing. Dressed as Wednesday, I'd offer them one. Instead of saying Wednesday's line, 'Go ahead. They're made from real Girl Scouts,' I said, 'Go ahead. They're made from real monsters.'"

Max laughed, "I can get behind that. Bullies deserve pay back."

"I had less flattering nicknames too, like Joyless, Black Death, or—and this one was actually pretty clever—students would walk by me and say, 'Hello, carry on.' but they meant 'carrion.' As a nickname—Carrion. Maybe that's why I shaved my head right before high school—to keep them away. I worked hard in school. I had to get out of there as fast as possible for survival sake. I showed them all up grade-wise. Sam put me in private after-school classes, and I left for college at fifteen. Sorry, that's bragging."

"Not if you did it to survive." The conversation lulled. Why had his father kept Joy and Sam Burton a secret? There was only one explanation, and he circled back to it: Max and Joy had been in foster care together, so it was natural that his father and hers had figured that they were too small to remember a bond with a foster sibling. No one "kept them apart." They just didn't put them together. David King adopted him and raised him. He rode ponies—and yes, he ran through the house with cowboy pistols and a cowboy hat and boots.

Max suddenly had a tough time reconciling the girl lecturing with authority and the girl holding the Glock with the vulnerable girl beside him now. Max asked, "Why do you have a man-eating snake?" He'd hoped to make Joy laugh, as he knew Monty could not eat a man. It worked. She chuckled but it was short-lived.

"Dad let me pick out a pet if I gave up my Shoebox of Horrors. I'm not sure what he thought when I picked Monty. After all, Monty eats dead things—and for the record—I mean 'dead' things—I don't feed her live animals."

"Would you feed Monty living things if you could?"

"No, both for ethical reasons and because live animals can injure Monty. I keep Monty's food—used to be mice, but now she eats rats—in the freezer."

"So, no dinner parties at your house."

Joy squinted her eyes in objection but continued, "Sam and I had a funeral and buried my shoe box. Sam understood me. And for that, I will always love him. But, Max, I don't understand me." Joy sat up and hugged her knees.

Max said, "Which led to your career choice."

"Psychology, sociology, forensics. And still, I don't understand the girl in the mirror."

Max stood up and stretched. He took off his shoes and slipped off his socks. He rolled up his pant legs and stepped into the water, letting it run over his toes. The image of David King's face, came at him. "Hold on there, Pride, Joy," David had said to them. What did Joy have to hold on to? He remembered how desperately she'd held onto him. But he woke up and he let her go. A pang of guilt punched his gut.

Before he knew it, Joy had rolled up her pant legs. She stepped in the stream beside him. "It really is lovely here."

"Look, Joy. I've made up my mind—"

"I know, Max. You don't have to—"

"Get the DNA kit from the car. I'll do it."

"What? You will?"

"One condition, though, and it's non-negotiable."

"Anything. I promise."

"Keep the results to yourself. No matter what you find, I don't want to know."

"I promise." Joy's lips swept into a bigger smile than Max had ever seen. He could see the weight that it pulled off of her shoulders. But it would not last. When the test came back negative for sibling status, it would crush her. If it came back otherwise, it would crush him—that's why he didn't want to know.

Then what? Could Joy let the past go and live in the present, or would she grab the shovel and keep digging until she found a skeleton? Max got out of the water and sat on the blanket.

Joy rushed back, tore open the kit, gave Max a vial, and

cautioned him not to do anything until she read the directions. "Okay, so it says we should not have eaten for at least thirty minutes. It's been at least that long since the coffee cake. We each spit until a vile, filling it up to the marked line."

"No cheek swab, huh?"

"This company runs a few other genetic tests while they're at it. Saliva is a larger sample size than a swab."

Max rallied up a gob of saliva and noisily spat into his vial. "You were going to talk my head off until I said yes, weren't you?"

"That was Plan A," said Joy, quietly trickling spit into her vial.

"Plan B?" *Spit.*

"Tie you to a chair. Put Monty around your neck, and when she constricted, and you screamed like a baby, I'd swab your cheek and go with another lab." *Spit.*

"Now that sounds like a Wednesday Addams kind of plan, you have to admit." *Spit.*

"Only if I enjoyed watching you choke." *Spit.*

Max eyed her sideways.

"Of course, I wouldn't. I'm not a homicidal maniac. I just dress like one."

"As we both know, Joy, they really do look 'just like everyone else.'"

18

M ax found seats at the Black Turtle Asian Bistro, while Joy mailed the DNA kit from the shipping store next door.

Max ordered food. The moment the waiter rushed away, Max's phone rang. "King."

"Are you sitting down?" asked Captain Banks.

"I am," said Max.

"According to Shane Drake's phone records, the last call he made was to Chief Goldsby's cell phone shortly before he died. The chief has been relieved of duty. Get over to his house and see if he has an alibi."

"Maybe Shane called the chief for help," defended Max.

"Shane didn't call 9-1-1, Max. He called the chief's private number. Stop by and get Goldsby's statement."

"Will do, captain."

Joy slid into the booth, and Max filled her in. "The last call Shane Drake made was to Chief Goldsby's cell. It's awfully sloppy. Maybe someone is framing him?"

Joy used a monotone Wednesday Addams voice. "Or he is trying to frame himself to look like he's being framed?"

After lunch, Max and Joy headed to the pharmacy where Shane had worked and spoke to his boss, Kirsten Jessen, a tall, middle-aged woman with glasses, who had never outgrown a ponytail.

Max showed her his credentials. "Please remember that our questions are strictly routine. Have you had any drugs go missing?"

Ms. Jessen sounded confident in her response. "If you mean narcotics, we keep them under lock and key. And, as you see, cameras are everywhere."

Joy added, "It sounds like Mr. Drake had chronic back pain."

"He did indeed," said Ms. Jessen, "but Shane knew exactly what he could take, when and how much. He never came to work in a stupor or groggy. Quite the opposite. He came in sometimes in severe pain, because he refused to be groggy on the job. Can you imagine if he put orders together incorrectly? The wrong pills in the wrong container? It could kill someone. Shane knew the outcome of addiction to pain relievers. He liked the night shift, because he could get off of his feet when he needed."

"Or he had fewer eyes on him," suggested Max.

Ms. Jessen seemed taken aback by the comment. "Shane had consulted a surgeon recently. He hated the idea of surgery, but he wanted to stop taking pain meds. He mentioned a girl. I think he had incentive." She paused, "I'll run an inventory to be sure."

Joy asked, "His doctor prescribed Fentanyl patches, is that right?"

"Let me see." Ms. Jessen stepped over to a computer and punched the keys. "Yes. In February. 100 micrograms. That's a high dose, but Shane had already been taking pain pills, so he'd built up some tolerance. That was around the time Shane suffered a new injury. Poor guy, he'd gone out for a walk to try to lose some weight, and he slipped on a wet patch on the sidewalk."

Joy asked, "How many patches to a box?"

"Five," said Ms. Jessen.

"Had he been acting strangely at all?" asked Max.

"I'm not on the night shift." Ms. Jessen's brows arched with worry. "I sure hope you're wrong—if you're implying misconduct." She paused. "Patients do create fake injuries to obtain medication. But I never once doubted Shane. Maybe I should have."

"We're just asking questions," said Joy. "We don't have the answers. Let us know what you find."

Max handed Ms. Jessen a card. "Here's the number." He added, "I need the name of the doctor who prescribed Mr. Drake's medications."

"Of course." Ms. Jessen wrote it down and handed it to Max.

On the way out, Joy surmised, "If Shane had three patches on his back, and there was one left in the box, then he'd only used one patch in six months—hardly the sign of an abuser."

"Or he bought his drugs on the street to avoid getting fired." Max unlocked the car and hopped in.

Joy buckled up.

Max said, "When I met with Eugene the second time, Shane drove past me on the way out. Eugene said they'd been toasting his engagement to Cynthia."

"Alcohol is a problem. Alcohol and pain meds are risky. Alcohol, pain meds, and three Fentanyl patches, lethal," said Joy.

A chill raced up Max's spine. "Joy, this is going to sound crazy, but the chief went ballistic when he found out that Shane knew about A-gamer."

"Yeah, I remember. He said he'd be ruined if it got out. You know him better than I do, Max. Do you think he'd go this far? Would he kill Anne and Shane to bury his dirty little secret?"

"Don't we all teeter on edges, Joy, between sane and insane, calm and crazed, lover and killer?" Max didn't have an answer, only more questions. Did the chief's fear of losing his career cause him to step over the line?

On the way to the chief's house, Max called the doctor, who confirmed Shane's struggle with pain meds. He worried that Shane stood dangerously close to addiction. He approved the Fentanyl prescription, but he also referred Shane to a surgeon with a stern warning he could not increase his meds any further. Max called the surgeon. Shane had made an appointment for the following week.

Max drove through the new housing development where the chief lived. Many of the houses on the block, including the chief's, had bare yards in need of landscaping. Maybe now, the chief had time to get after the details that made a tract house a home—if anyone could call his mini-French chateau a tract home. Max could imagine the chief living in an English Tudor or an American craftsmen, but never in a mini-country estate in France. The chief didn't seem that elegant or refined. Cast a wide net, Max reminded himself. Like any other suspect, Max needed to see the chief as he was and let his prejudices go. It did make Max smile to think the chief had a foofy side, though.

Max and Joy sidestepped a box from a home shopping network. Max picked it up.

When the chief opened the door, Max saw two expressions on the his face: one begrudgingly welcomed him and the other despised his presence. Max and Joy followed the chief inside. Max set the box on the tiled floor.

The chief had once tried to scuttle Max's career with what

he later called an initiation, a test of character. He sent Max on a witness interview and had a vice officer try to seduce him. Max arrested her. She didn't mention who she was until the chief cut her loose at the station, and she said, "Congratulations on making detective."

Max had no sympathy for the chief or for the fact that his career sat on the chopping block, but unlike the chief, he would fight for justice. If the chief was innocent, he'd prove it and clear his name. If he was guilty, he'd make sure the chief paid for his crimes.

The chief sat in an extra-wide hunter green chair, while Max and Joy sat on the matching sofa.

"Lovely home, chief," said Joy. "How are you holding up?"

"How do you think? I'm not! What have you found?" The chief relit a cigar sitting in an ashtray on the side table next to him.

Max cut to the chase. "Chief, to be blunt, we're not here to give you a report. You're a suspect, and Joy and I need to rule you out."

The chief puffed on his cigar. "Shoot. What do you need from me?" Thick swirls of sweet smoke snaked into the air.

Joy asked, "Did you speak to Shane Drake yesterday?"

The chief responded rather quickly, "No, why?"

"You're sure?" asked Max. "Take your time."

The chief's voice rose three notches. "I don't need more time! I didn't speak to—wait, the phone rang last night. I was sitting right here. Just lit this very same cigar and had a glass of Merlot. I picked up the call, but no one answered. Caller ID said it was Shane."

Joy let out an audible sigh. "No alibi, then? Did you have any company, chief?"

"No." The chief looked perplexed. "Who would do this to me? Never mind, I can think of plenty who would. Did you talk to A-gamer?"

Max could not answer any of the chief's questions, but he could ask more questions. "We've put surveillance on him. Who else hates you enough to pin two murders on you?"

"I don't have a clue. The list is long," said Goldsby.

The chief's jowls hung lower than Max had ever seen. His eyes were dark circles. His white hair hadn't been brushed. A lock of it stuck up on one side. The chief hadn't shaved. Authority and anger had kept him flushed and taut while on the job, but sitting at home had sucked the wind out of his sails, and his face sagged in defeat. The chief puffed quietly on his cigar like a man having his last smoke, determined to enjoy every moment and morsel of flavor. "I've been around here a long time. Only been chief three years, but I've arrested plenty of criminals. Riled even more."

Joy leaned forward. "Chief, when did you see your cigar cutter last?"

"At the game. I didn't even know it was missing until the next day."

Max asked, "When was the last time you were at Shane Drake's house?"

"When he hosted the poker game. We had five regulars, but we're open to guests, like when you came, Max, with your dad some years back or when Deon came."

"That was a few years ago. Different cast of characters than when I played," said Max.

"Right,' said the chief. "I bumped into Anne at a hospital charity dinner. She was with Grant, and I happened to sit at their table. They invited me to join their poker group. But to answer your question, Eugene hosted this month, Lee hosted last month, Grant hosted June, then it was me, and then Anne —but her place is so small, we met at Grant's house—and Shane would have hosted in March."

Joy sighed. "So you haven't been to Shane's house in several months?"

"Right," said the chief. "That's good, I hope."

Max pursed his lips in frustration. "Did Shane smoke cigars? Did you give him one to smoke on poker night?" Max's brain wanted to solve this riddle. He fought to find other plausible solutions. There had to be one.

The chief answered in a combative tone. "Shane smoked an occasional cigar. Cynthia preferred that we smoke outside. But Eugene let that go on poker night at his house. Except for Grant. He lights up cigarettes end to end. Cynthia made him smoke outside."

Max asked, "Did Shane smoke at the poker game?"

The chief leaned forward in his chair. "What the hell did you find at Shane's, another cigar clipper? Tell me!"

"A cigar butt," said Max. "Your brand. Half smoked."

The chief slipped into police mode. "My saliva or Shane's?"

"Don't know yet," said Max.

The chief barked, "If it's mine, someone wants to land my butt in jail! And they're succeeding." The chief jumped up and paced the taupe carpet. "It was hot. We left the patio doors open to get some air. After we left, anyone could have slipped in and stolen the butt I left behind. A-gamer hated me and Anne."

Pictures of French landscapes, vineyards, and cafes leaned against the walls, waiting for someone to put them in place. The peaceful rustic pictures contrasted sharply with Chief Goldsby's fears and his flushed face.

"Deon said he'd never played with the group before. Is that true?" asked Max.

"Yes," said the chief. "But he knew Anne and possibly Grant." The chief set his cigar in the ashtray. He grabbed a half empty bottle of Merlot from the end table, poured a slosh into a glass, and gulped it down. "My nerves can't take this."

Joy offered unwanted advice. "Keep your wits. Don't make it worse."

"Keep my wits!" Chief Goldsby clutched the wine glass and

bottle like a drowning man clutched a flotation device. "I'm losing my mind. I feel helpless."

"We'll re-interview the witnesses. Someone must have seen something that can help us." Max rose to leave. "We'll figure this out."

The chief poured himself a full glass of wine. "Before I'm tossed in the can would be preferable."

The moment Max stepped outside, his bravado left him. "This case doesn't make any sense! I'm half thinking the chief did do it. Maybe that was all an act."

Joy laughed.

Max shot her a glare of defiance. "What's so funny?"

"Think of any case you've ever been on or assisted with, Max. Even if you were pretty sure you knew who did it..."

Max finished the sentence. "...it never makes sense until it makes sense. David King."

Joy said, "Sam Burton."

19

The next day, Joy showed up at the station with a bag in-hand. She set it before Max. "Jayda clued me in to your crumble and glazed donut fetish. I feel like I muscled you yesterday. Truce." She pulled up a chair and sat down.

Max reached for the bag. "To make a truce, you have to have a war. We didn't. But I gladly accept your donuts."

Kevin approached Max and Joy, escorting a woman. "Max, this is Lisa Nguyen. She says she has information regarding the Anne Martin case."

"We met at the hospital," said Max, already pulling up another chair. "Please."

Ms. Nguyen wore blue scrubs. As she sat, she set a white purse in her lap. "This is probably nothing, but I got to thinking maybe it would help. I told my husband, and he said I had to come see you. He said what if it helps and I said nothing. So here I am."

"What is it?" asked Max.

Ms. Nguyen took a deep breath. "A little over eight months ago—I checked the hospital database to be sure—Anne had an accident. That's what she said, 'an accident.' She broke her wrist. She took a couple of weeks off work, and when she came back, she had to be on desk duty until the doctor cleared her for floor duty."

"It wasn't an accident?" asked Joy.

Ms. Nguyen pointed to her cheek. "Anne had bruises on her face. She said she'd fallen down some stairs, but, well, I'm a nurse. I've seen the signs. This wasn't Anne's first 'accident.'" She pulled back. "Anne and Dr. Grant—they have history. Dr. Grant...well, I've never seen him as an abuser until then. Something happened."

Joy asked, "Did Anne have accidents on a regular basis?"

Ms. Nguyen protested. "No. That's why I didn't say anything. But my husband said, maybe Anne hid it well or maybe Dr. Grant escalated. I don't see Anne staying with a man who hit her. She didn't live with him. They tried that a time or two, but she always went back to her house. I mean, she seemed happy most of the time. But not this year. Something changed."

Joy pressed her. "You think Dr. Grant broke Anne's wrist?"

Ms. Nguyen glanced at the floor. Max and Joy gave her time. Witnesses felt guilty if they gave inaccurate information or falsely slandered someone, but without leads to follow, pieces of the puzzle remained missing.

Max said, "Anything you tell us might just be the clue to finding out what happened to Anne."

Ms. Nguyen nodded and straightened her shoulders. She glanced between Max and Joy and spoke with assurance. "Anne gave me the number of an old friend she'd planned on visiting for a few days while she recuperated. She seemed nervous about anyone but me knowing where she went. She made me promise not to give the number to Dr. Grant or to anyone else." Mrs. Nguyen reached into her purse and pulled out a piece of paper. Anne had written the name "Hammer" and a phone number.

Max took the note. Nothing stirred cops' blood more than a

new lead, because each one could be the piece needed to break a case. "You did the right thing. Thank you for coming in."

Mrs. Nguyen rose to her feet. "I miss Anne. She never said 'no' when someone needed help. I forgot all about that number. I was digging in my purse yesterday, and there it was. Like Anne wanted you to have it. Is that silly?"

Joy shook her head. "The dead talk to me all the time. To Detective King too. But not everyone, like you, stops to listen."

Ms. Nguyen nodded. "I appreciate your saying so. I'm glad I came in."

After she left, Max commented, making a reference to his middle name. "Hammer? And I thought 'Pride' was a weird name."

"It is," said Joy. "It's a little arrogant."

"We're talking about the name Hammer, right?"

Joy smirked. "Of course, Pride."

Max and Joy drove to Lake Elsinore, a town situated around a small lake nestled in the Santa Ana Mountain range and bordered by Temescal Canyon and Temescal Mountains. The town had stayed small from its 1800s inception until about 1980, when it had fewer than six thousand residents. After that, it exploded to ten times that number when developers swarmed the area.

Max drove through an older section of town. The homes, a combination of ramshackle and spruced up, sat on decent-sized pieces of unkempt land.

One house stood out. It had fresh white paint with yellow and green trim. The front yard was manicured dirt, decorative rocks, and drought-tolerant plants. Some plants sat in brightly colored Talavera pots, similar to the ones at Anne's house, only much bigger.

Max knocked on the green door, hand-painted with bright yellow sunflowers.

A Hispanic woman, mid-thirties, opened the door. "Can I help you?"

"I'm Detective Max King, and this is Dr. Joy Burton. Does Nico Torres live here?"

"That's my husband. He's working, but I can give you his cell phone number. Is there a problem?"

"No," said Max. "We just have a few questions about a friend of his."

Once back in the car, Joy confirmed the number the woman provided matched the one on the note, not that they had a doubt.

Max punched the numbers into his phone. As soon as he heard, "Hello," Max said, "This is Detective Max King of the Wine Valley PD. I'm calling in reference to Anne Martin. My partner and I are in Lake Elsinore. Can we meet?"

Nico Torres hesitated but ultimately offered a location for a meetup.

20

Max and Joy strolled into a Mexican restaurant in the heart of town. The place was brightly painted inside—yellow, salmon, and green. Colorful sombreros hung from the walls, like guests could grab one and start dancing to the music being played.

Nico had medium-length dark hair pulled back in a pony-tail, a thick mustache, strong facial features, and determined dark blue eyes. He sipped on a Coke, eyeing the door. It was early and the only other customers were an elderly couple.

Max slid into a seat. Joy sat beside him. Max said, "Thanks for meeting with us, Mr. Torres."

Nico asked, "How did you find me?"

Joy answered, "Anne's nursing supervisor had your number, but the name was 'Hammer.'"

Nico smiled. "That's a nickname. My wife hates it, but the guys in my bike club use it. Annie knew me by that name." The man leaned back. "God. That was a long time ago. I was a handyman—hence the name Hammer—not as dramatic as you probably thought. I did a lot of work helping Annie's dad fix up his home. Annie and I grew up here. Went to school together. Hung out."

Max asked, "You dated?"

Nico leaned forward and rested his forearms on the table. "She ran away with me. See, her father thought I was good enough to do his carpentry work but not good enough for his pretty white daughter. He said she was made for better things than the likes of me. Her old man lived in a pre-fab in a trailer park, but he told me that with her looks, she could live in a mansion. But Annie chose me. Her dad said he wouldn't speak to her as long as she was with me. I helped pay her way through nursing school. She commuted to Wine Valley for work."

"It sounds like you were both happy," said Joy.

"We were," said Nico. "Annie pushed me to take night classes to get my contractor's license. She had patience with me. She'd spend hours helping me study for the exams. She never made me feel dumb. It took some doing, but I got my license, and I started my own company. During my last semester, she met the doctor."

"Dr. Grant," confirmed Joy.

Nico nodded. "If I had a night class, Annie sometimes stopped at a local 50s diner in Wine Valley and ate dinner at the counter before coming home. Grant saw her there one night and swooped in. He bought her dinner, found out she worked at the hospital. He just couldn't leave her alone, leave us alone. We had plans. One day, we took a walk, and Annie spotted this run-down little house. I promised her I'd buy it for us and fix it up. And I did, just not for her. 'Bout a month before graduation, I asked Annie to marry me. I told her we could start a family. She said to wait until I graduated. But she was just waiting for the right time to leave." Nico sipped his Coke. "Did you meet Dr. Grant?"

"Yes," said Max.

Nico's eyes glared with pure hate. "Did he tell you he was the one who got Annie into gambling?"

Max and Joy eyed one another.

"I thought not." Nico leaned back. His voice rose a notch. "Grant flashed money before her eyes. He took her to the casino and taught her how to play poker, Black Jack, Roulette. Annie took to poker like a duck to water. I couldn't compete with flashy cars and luxury houses."

"You stayed in touch?" asked Joy.

"For a while," said Nico. "He bought that small house by the creek for her—but he never put it in her name. One day, I went there to try to bring her home. Grant showed up. He said the same thing as her father, that she deserved better than what I could give her. Maybe Annie finally believed it too." Nico grinned. "Before I left, though, I clocked Grant, real hard. And I don't regret it. That was the last time I spoke to Annie, until last December when she called out of the blue."

Max asked, "When she broke her wrist?"

Nico nodded. "She told me she and Grant got into a fight. She broke up. For good. She said she just wanted to talk, like old times. My wife and kids had taken off for Mexico to visit with her family over the Christmas holidays, but I had a big job, so I couldn't go. I guess I was curious. I told Annie to drive up. It was a mistake." Nico reached for his Coke and sucked it back as if needing the icy cold slap and caffeine and sugar before going on.

Max asked, "How did she react seeing the house and you?"

"She didn't even make it to the front door. She sank to her knees in the dirt and she cried and cried. I've seen some broken people in my time, but man, Annie. It was like she'd kept so many secrets for so long, they all came tumbling out at once. She told me how Grant had introduced her to gambling. How she'd gambled away what her father had left her. She was in debt to the casino. She and Grant fought. Grant grabbed her arm. She twisted away from him and fell. She landed with her arm pinned beneath her. She broke her wrist and sprained her shoulder. She had a bruised cheek too, like he'd hit her. She begged me to help her. She asked me for a loan. Twenty grand." Nico shook his head. "I told her I didn't have it, and even if I did, I had a family to support. An alcoholic can't drink a little, a drug addict can't take a small hit, and I knew Annie had a gambling problem."

"Why did she call you? It had been a long time," asked Joy.

Nico shrugged. "Maybe I reminded her of better times. I told her to get an advance from the hospital or a friend. She didn't want the hospital knowing she had money problems. She said Grant had cut her off financially, even told her that if she left him, she had to start paying rent on the cottage. He was like that. He kept her needing him. Annie said he was jealous, possessive. She said she never should have left me. Said it was the worst mistake of her life. She made a pass at me, said we could start over. I grabbed her shoulders and pushed her back, but gentle, you know, because she had her arm in a sling. I told her the truth—I didn't want her back. I love my wife. I love my kids. I told her to leave the doctor, pay off the debt, get help, and find a good man. I asked her to leave."

"Did you give her any money?" asked Joy.

Nico hesitated. He dropped his chin to his chest in defeat. "Five hundred. She promised she'd pay me back. Said she could win it back, even pay me interest. I knew I'd never see it. She got in her car and left. I never heard from her after that. Then I see on the news she's dead. I bet Grant did it."

"Why didn't you call us?" asked Max.

Nico sucked down the rest of his Coke and pushed the ice-filled glass away. "I didn't know Annie anymore. I couldn't add any information that would help. At least, that's what I thought." Nico leaned forward and dropped his voice to a whisper. "Besides, if my wife found out, she'd kick my ass from here to the Panama Canal."

Max handed Nico a card. "Call us if you think of anything else."

Nico said with urgency, "You're not going to talk to my wife, are you?"

Joy assured him, "We stopped by your house but said we had a question about an acquaintance of yours. We didn't specify beyond that."

Max said, "I think we can keep this out of the Canal Zone."

On the way back to town, Max saw Anne—or Annie— from a new perspective, an image forged by her father, a man with bigoted beliefs that had pushed his daughter into the arms of a man that would please *him*—handsome, rich and white—even if it led to her ruin and, ultimately, to her death.

Had her father's conviction that Anne deserved more nudged her to leave Hammer and run to Grant? Or had the cash and cars tempted her with promises of a rich life? And was her pass at Nico genuine or an attempt to do anything to solve her money problems?

No wonder Anne set money on the table, hoping to hit it big. Compulsive gamblers believed they could beat the odds— but the odds were always against them. The house always won.

Max imagined Anne's life had she made another choice. He could picture her with Hammer, living in the colorful little house. Anne would still be a nurse helping people. Hammer would remodel homes, and they'd take walks and motorcycle rides, raise kids, and laugh.

On the other hand, Anne's dark side was present all along. Impulsivity. The cravings. She'd gambled on Hammer when she ran away with him. She gambled again when she ran to

Grant. Gambling came easy. "Let's get Grant inside the station and in the line of fire. It might shake him up enough to get at the truth. He's been holding back."

"I totally agree," said Joy. "We know his Achilles heel—Anne. Let's stop by Belle's first. It's lunch time."

Max seemed surprised. "Is my food obsession rubbing off on you?"

"More like a Belle obsession. She makes a killer shake, she's adorable, and I'm hungry."

"She makes everything from scratch, even the BBQ sauce. It wouldn't surprise me if she could aim a Glock."

"No, Max. Belle is a rifle girl. I'd bet lunch on it."

Max scolded, "Have we learned nothing about the ills of gambling? Besides, I'm not dumb enough to bet against a profiler's daughter."

Max and Joy escorted Dr. Grant to an interrogation room. The new station still smelled of carpet glue and paint.

The building also had the newest technology. The interrogation room had one-way glass, a TV screen on a wall mount in the upper corner, and multiple cameras—all of which added an intimidation factor. The technology reminded suspects and witnesses of the modern-day methods by which the police obtained evidence.

Max and Joy sat opposite Dr. Grant.

Grant set his cigarettes and lighter on the table. "Can I smoke?"

Max's father sometimes allowed a suspect to smoke to get on his good side or to get him relaxed—even after California passed the ban on smoking in public buildings. Max preferred to keep Grant on edge—and under his thumb. "Sorry. No smoking in public buildings."

Grant asked, "Why am I here?"

Max asked, "Did you and Anne have a fight, one that led to injury in December?"

Grant's face and neck muscles grew tense. "Yes, we fought. She'd just gotten cut off from the casino, and she wanted me to front her money so she could win it back. I told you that."

"You failed to mention that you broke her wrist," accused Joy.

"It was more her fault than mine," said Grant. "She reached for my wallet. I grabbed her wrist. She slapped me. I reacted. I slapped her back, harder than I realized. She twisted away from me and fell backwards. She landed with her arm under her. I was trying to get her to listen to reason. She was out of control."

Joy replied with unmistakable sarcasm. "*She* was out of control?"

Grant shot forward and slapped both palms on the table. "I loved her!"

Max looked at Joy. "Funny way to show it."

Joy used a soft, melodic voice, like that of a snake charmer. "It must have been difficult for you to watch her gamble away her inheritance. For you to try to stop her from gambling."

Grant folded his arms across his chest in defiant obstinance. "You have no idea!"

Max confronted Grant. "Except that we heard you taught Anne to gamble."

Grant's face imploded. He ran his hands over the top of his head. His chest heaved. He struggled to regain composure and stymie the guilt and anger and emotions that threatened to spill over. He eyed the pack of cigarettes. "Just let me have a smoke, and I'll answer your questions. Please."

Max nodded.

Grant's hands shook as he shoved a cigarette between his lips, lit the end, and inhaled a deep drag. He rose to his feet, as if to exhale his dirty air farther away from non-smokers. "I still can't kick these filthy things." He took another long drag, this time exhaling at a calmer rate. "I didn't see it coming. We laughed and had fun at the casino. We danced, ate good food.

Do you have any idea how guilty I feel, an addict giving an addiction to another human being?" Grant's voice rumbled with deep-seated pain. "How about that for luck and love? I used women right and left. I admit it, but I fell in love with Anne, and it all falls apart. Anne was a small-town girl. So sweet. But she liked the lights, the money. Two addicts. We never stood a chance." Grant sucked in a deep lungful of smoke, dropped the cigarette to the floor, and stomped on the burning end.

Max said calmly, "Sit down, Dr. Grant."

Grant dropped into the chair, a broken man. "She's gone. I'll never see her again."

Joy offered him some solace. "We all gamble to some degree. We buy a lotto ticket or enter a raffle or we bet a friend who will win a sporting event. But gambling addicts either struggle with severe financial problems or enjoy the thrill and adrenaline of taking risks. They get in deeper and see gambling as the only way out. Anne had some component within her that triggered the addiction. We can't escape our DNA." Joy shot a glance at Max.

Max wondered if Joy spoke about Grant, Anne, or herself. It was time to press Grant. "Anne disappeared after the wrist incident. She went home to her old boyfriend."

"Hammer?" asked Grant. "He broke my nose. I deserved it, though. I'd have done the same to him."

Max leaned across the table. "Anne told him everything. How you cut her off financially. She described you as possessive and jealous. He told her to leave you and find a good man. Looks like she was working to do both."

Grant's anger flared. "Anne made idle threats! She always came back to me. She knows how I get sometimes. And I know her. We were meant to be together."

"You strung her along, made her desperate and dependent," accused Joy.

Grant slammed a fist on the table. "Addiction makes you desperate and dependent! I was trying to help her, damn it!"

"Did she mention A-gamer?" asked Max.

Grant's blood boiled. "Who's that? Another lover?"

"A loan shark," said Joy, pulling a picture out of a folder. "Do you recognize him?"

"A loan shark? Jesus, Anne!" Grant eyed the mug shot. "Never seen him." Grant's shoulders sagged. "I would have married her. Paid her debt and gone to meetings with her. But when she came back, she said I had ruined her life—she blamed me! She said she was done with me. I thought it was just a ploy to get me to pay her debt. For once, I didn't give in. I'd bailed her out so many times before."

"Is that why you confronted her at the poker game?" accused Max. "She didn't come back this time, so you waited for her? Hit her. Killed her."

Grant snapped. "No!"

"You don't remember," Joy reminded him.

"I would never hurt— " Grant's face twisted with torment. He nervously rubbed his knuckles. "I think I might have hit her, but I didn't kill her. I wouldn't...I could never..."

Max rose to his feet so fast, his chair grated against the stained concrete floor as he shoved it back. He had no sympathy for an abuser, and Grant had just let slip one confession. It was time to get the rest. Max slammed his palms on the table and leaned over. "She dumped you, for good!"

Grant protested. "She always came back."

Joy goaded him, "Not this time. She slept with Eug—"

Grant raised his voice. "She was confused. That's all."

"You kept her confused," argued Max, "but she started to see clearly, and she saw that you were the problem!"

"That's not true. I helped her!" shouted Grant.

"Did you kill her for walking away?" asked Joy.

"No!" said Grant.

"For going to see her old boyfriend and throwing herself at him?" asked Max.

Grant's eyes flashed wide. "I didn't know about that until you told me!"

"She used you, like you used her?" accused Joy.

Grant pleaded, "I loved her! More than I've ever loved anybody."

"And she broke it off!" reminded Joy.

Max paced the floor. "You were drunk. You went back. You pounded on Anne's door. She didn't answer. You followed the path and confronted her. You lost your temper, struck her. She fell in the water. You panicked."

Joy added, "Did you caress her hair, ready to apologize, but your hand held her down instead?"

Grant shook his head. "No! You're wrong. I couldn't. Not to Anne."

Joy reminded him, "You're an addict, Dr. Grant. Anne was your addiction, your obsession. If you couldn't have her, no one could. Did she tell you about Eugene, throw it in your face, or did you guess?"

Grant leaped out of his chair as if to run away, but he had no where to go. He leaned against the wall. "I didn't kill her! Maybe I did push Anne too hard; maybe I wasn't helping her, just driving her deeper. Maybe she realized I'm an ass. If she loved Eugene enough to stop gambling, enough to start a new life, then I would have been happy for her."

Joy objected, "If that were true, you wouldn't have fallen off the wagon and stalked her. Or hit her."

Max had heard enough. Grant had motive and opportunity. He confronted Anne—by his own admission. "Dr. Grant, we're holding you. So get comfy."

Dr. Grant glanced up at Max. Anger filled his eyes. He transformed into Mr. Hyde. He grabbed the chair and hurled it against the wall, letting out a feral yell.

Officers rushed in, threw the doctor up against the wall, cuffed him, and dragged him away.

Back at his desk, Max admitted, "I'm not buying his love story?"

As Joy sat in a chair beside Max, she offered an explanation. "That part I believe. Most batterers say they love their spouses. He loved Anne, but he also needed to control her. Anne got under his skin. He fell for her, but he couldn't control her gambling or her flirtatious nature. If he found out about her foray with Eugene, he had plenty of motive. Maybe he suspected Shane was a lover too."

Max leaned forward like he had an idea. "Maybe Goldsby wasn't targeted because anyone had a vendetta against him. Maybe he was simply a convenient scapegoat. He lives alone, so most likely, he wouldn't have an alibi after the game. The killer just needed to know his habits. The Chens, as well as Eugene and Cynthia, reside with others. Shane, Grant, Deon, and Goldsby reside alone."

"Interesting logic, Max. Why not frame Grant?" asked Joy. "Or Deon?" "You know him better than I do, Max. Is Goldsby that clever? Would he incriminate himself?""

Max pondered the question. "He knows procedure. He might be playing the system—and us."

"But it's risky," said Joy. "If he killed Anne to protect himself from the A-gamer story getting out, and if he killed Shane because he knew the real story, Goldsby might just end up in jail."

"No," said Max. "It's circumstantial evidence. It's brilliant. He can say he's being framed. There are too many other suspects."

Max's cell phone rang. "King." Max listened. His eyes lit up. "We're on the way." He hung up. "Deon just showed up at The Stinky Mule."

22

By the time Max and Joy arrived, the surveillance team had wired Reed Steele, a scrappy, undercover officer with long, chestnut brown hair, a mustache, and a day's worth of stubble. His hazel eyes projected mental toughness, as did his square jaw. He dressed in scruffy jeans, a gray T-shirt that hugged his muscular chest and shoulders, and a biker vest.

"Who's your new partner?" asked Steele, eyeing Joy.

"Dr. Joy Burton," said Max. "Joy, this is Reed Steele."

"Doctor?" said Steele. "I think I'm feeling ill."

Joy shot Reed her deadpan Wednesday Addam's face and monotone voice. "If you're sick in the head, I can help."

"I'll bet you could drive me crazy." Steele raised his eyebrows.

"Well, I'm already there: criminally insane." Joy said this in such a serious tone, Steele stopped laughing.

Max grinned, "She's not kidding. How's our boy?"

"Your guy seems nervous," said Steele. "He sat in his car for a good half hour. He just went in."

"Maybe he's thinking twice after talking to me at the hospital," suggested Max.

Joy added, "He may or may not know the hospital is aware of the missing drugs."

"Or he doesn't think anyone is watching," said Max. "They never do. Even if we're onto them—criminals just can't stop being criminals."

"You're live, Steele," said Riggs, the station computer nerd and tech specialist who had set the wires in place. Nathan wore glasses, which heightened his nerdy appearance. He often, like now, tried too hard to compensate. He focused on Steele and the mission, but his eyes diverted to Joy a time or two, like a teenager noticing a girl for the first time. "Got a code word for storming the castle?"

Steele smirked. "Joy ride." He turned away and headed to the bar.

"Tell me he doesn't think that was cute or adorable," Joy said with a tone of mock disgust.

Max laughed. "Steele's a good cop. He worked the gang beat in Los Angeles. Moved here after he was shot a second time. Let's take the back." Max headed to the rear of the building. Joy followed.

"I have to admit, it was rather witty," said Joy. "Not adorable, mind you. But witty."

"You like him. Probably because he's been shot up a couple of times. He's damaged like you."

"And you are a relationship expert because..."

Max laughed. "Joy ride. I mean, it's perfectly innocent on one hand and so wrong on the other."

Joy allowed herself a half smile. "I know."

Weapons drawn, Max and Joy flanked the back door of the bar and waited for the signal.

Steele sat at the end of the bar and ordered a beer. He spotted Deon in A-gamer's corner near the pool tables. Deon exchanged a package for an envelope and stuffed the envelope inside the waistband of his pants under his shirt.

One of A-gamer's boys, a fat white kid with greasy, dyed, blond hair, stepped to the bar and ordered a couple of beers. He blocked Steele's view and struck up a conversation. "Do I know you?"

"No," said Steele. "Let's keep it that way."

The kid whipped out a switchblade. "See, this is kind of an exclusive place. No one comes in here unless you're on the guest list. Name?"

"First name is Piss. Last name is Off." Steele pulled out a bigger blade and popped it open under the bar. "Dude, I don't know your game, but I'm gonna finish my beer, and then you can have your country club all to yourself again."

"Who's your crew?"

Steele sipped his beer. "Was M8." Steele referred to Mixteca 8, the gang that had killed his brother in gang crossfire when he and Dante were kids. Steel added, "I left LA after the shoot out at Otero's place."

The fat boy's eyes grew wide and his jaw dropped. "Man, you were there? That's legend! Piss Off, come meet my friends. You might like to join the country club. I'm Wall." The greasy-haired kid put his knife away and grabbed the two beers the bartender had set on the counter. He headed to the pool tables.

Steele put his blade away. "I might." Beer in hand, Steele followed Wall, an appropriate name for the monolith who escorted him to the back of the room.

Deon aimed his cue stick. He struck the white ball. It connected with the solid purple ball, which rolled to the corner pocket and fell in. "Can't catch me!" Deon swigged his beer before lining up his next shot, having moved from nervousness to bravado.

"A-gamer, meet..." Wall waited for a real name.

"Ice," said Steele.

Wall added, "He's M8. From LA."

Steele corrected, "Was M8."

A-gamer's eyes drifted to Steele. "Long ways from home."

"Looking for a new home." Steele lifted his shirt to show a scar that ran from the tip of his sternum, down his abdomen, and dove beneath the waistline of his jeans.

A-gamer bobbed his head in admiration. "Nice buck-fifty." He used the term for one-hundred fifty stitches, a street term for a life-threatening wound.

Upon seeing the scar, Deon missed his next shot.

"Scars are only nice if you live to talk about 'em," said Steele, lowering his shirt. "With Otero gone, I figure I'd move south before the cops blew off my dick."

Deon reverted to his former jittery state. "Hey, you guys have company, so I'll take off. I forfeit the game."

Steele leaned against the table to block Deon's exit. "This dude looks nervous. Like a cop."

A-gamer laughed. "Nah, he's harmless."

"I can smell a cop." Steel sniffed the air near Deon's head. "This guy smells like DEA."

A-gamer grinned. "He's a nurse."

"Sweet! A pipeline," said Steele, slapping A-gamer on the shoulder. "We had a few of those. Nurses with needs."

A-gamer leaned over the table to take a shot. "He's a real entrepreneur. Followed his friend here, and when she quit, he signed on."

"Anything I'd be interested in?" asked Steele.

"512s and z-bars, this time," said A-gamer, using street names for oxycodone and Xanax. "He can do better."

Deon shot A-gamer a cross look. "Not with admin breathing down my neck."

"You said 'she' quit. We don't let 'em quit in L.A." Steele motioned across his neck. "But they can leave in peace."

A-gamer smirked. "First, she got cold feet. Then the rest of her got real cold."

"I hope you got a 'joy ride' first?" Steele had heard enough. He gave the signal.

A-gamer and his boys broke out laughing.

"Hey, Anne was my friend." Deon made a move to leave, but Steele blocked his exit with his body and narrowed eyes, daring him to skirt around him.

In seconds, Max and Joy burst through the back door, Glocks drawn. Two uniforms rushed through the front entrance.

"Freeze, police!" shouted Max.

Steele threw his hands in the air while looking for the package that Deon had handed to A-gamer and A-gamer had handed to one of his boys. He was too smart to get caught holding it himself. Wall dropped the package to the floor and kicked it beneath his chair.

Deon reached for the envelope he'd stuffed down his pants, but Max pointed his Glock at him, and Deon froze. "Don't move a muscle, Deon."

Deon's face grimaced with shock and fear. He rolled his eyes skyward as if pleading for help, but knowing it was too late for that.

More from instinct than a well thought-out plan, Wall whipped out his switchblade and swiped the air.

Joy pointed her Glock at him. "Dude, you seriously want to go against my Glock with that pencil?"

Wall dropped the blade.

A-gamer stayed calm. His eyes roved up and down Joy's body. "If it isn't Sweet-cheeks? I knew you'd be back for more." He put his hands behind his head and stretched. "I'm ready. Come frisk me."

Joy aimed her Glock at A-gamer's head. "You can call me Badass. Now that we've been introduced, how about you frisk my barrel and see if you get a happy ending?"

Max led Steele out in cuffs to maintain the illusion and keep his undercover identity intact. On the way out the front door, following behind the others, Steele whispered to Max, "I think I'm in love with Badass."

Max cautioned, "I'd take her at her word about the criminally insane thing."

23

Max and Joy stuffed Deon in the back seat, and he whimpered the entire way back to the station. They decided to let A-gamer stew in another room while they interrogated Deon first.

Joy tossed the package of drugs and the envelope full of money on the table, both in evidence bags, and slid into a seat opposite Deon.

Max paced the room, circling Deon like a vulture waiting for a bloody scent, ready to dive in and catch his prey.

Joy clasped her hands and set them on the table. "Looks like we found our hospital drug thief? 512s and Z-bars this time."

Deon's face contorted in angst. "Look, hear me. I was just in the wrong place at the wrong time. Just playin' a game of pool."

"With your pants stuffed full of money?" asked Max.

"I...I...won a game," said Deon. "Lucky me."

Max circled. "So your prints won't be on those drugs?"

Joy added, "And A-gamer as much as admitted you were his supplier."

"No, the long-haired dude, Ice, said that," argued Deon. "I don't even know that guy."

Max leaned over, practically breathing down Deon's neck. "Help us out, Deon. We're looking for Anne's killer. This is small potatoes. It helps to cooperate."

Deon ran his hands over his face to wipe the sweat from his brow. "Anne was his supplier. I saw her take some meds one day, and I followed her to The Stinky Mule. I came inside and hid in a dark spot at the end of the bar. She gave an envelope to A-gamer. She said they were square. Said she regretted the day she ever met him. He said she still owed him. He tried to make a move on her, and she slapped him—real hard. His boys were about to move on her, but in walks this white-haired, pudgy cop. As soon as Anne sees him, she leaves. Then the cop tells A-gamer that her account is closed, permanently, or he'll hunt him down and toss him behind bars if he so much as jaywalks."

Joy asked, "Would you recognize the cop?"

Deon answered quickly. "Sure. White hair, pale skin, red cheeks, not real tall."

Joy opened a manila folder. She shoved a picture of the chief in front of Deon.

"Yeah, that's him," said Deon.

"Frank Goldsby," Joy said for the record. She left out his title. "Did the cop make a deal with A-gamer? Did he give or receive any packages?"

Deon shook his head. "He said what he had to say and split."

"Did Anne see you?" asked Max. "Maybe you were afraid she'd tattle about your arrangement with A-gamer or turn you in for stealing drugs."

Deon waved his hands in the air, like he tried frantically to stop a train. "That ain't it! I couldn't believe she was selling drugs. Why did she do that?"

"She liked to gamble." Max continued to pace. "She borrowed money from A-gamer."

"A-gamer probably killed her then!" Deon squirmed in his seat. He leaned forward as if trying to help solve the crime. "He said so, didn't he? He said something like that? About her feet getting cold? I'll cooperate. I swear."

Max confirmed, "So, you didn't see the white-haired cop in A-gamer's presence except this once?"

"Right," said Deon. "Just the one time."

Joy asked, "And the cop, Frank Goldsby, did't have any other business with A-gamer that you know of?"

"No. Like I said, he just made a threat," said Deon.

Joy asked, "So, after Anne and the cop left, you made an arrangement with A-gamer to pick up where Anne left off?"

Deon let out a single whimper.

Max said, "We have a reliable witness who saw you make the exchange with A-gamer, the package with the drugs for the package with the money. Why did you do it?"

Deon grimaced with the anticipation of the hardships to come. "To pay back my student loans, you know. They're hanging over my head. My folks didn't have the money for college. Dumb! I'm so dumb! I almost chickened out today." Deon shuddered with remorse and sobbed into his hands.

Max and Joy exchanged a look of compassion. Sometimes, people just screwed up. They didn't think it through. Neither Max nor Joy could say a word, but they both knew a good attorney would plea-bargain for a lesser offense. Deon's testimony could clear the chief of police of any wrongdoing, at least with the incident involving Anne. And Deon could help convict A-gamer for drug trafficking, although A-gamer's attorney would shred the testimony of a drug supplier who'd made a deal with the DA. Still, those chips were valuable, and a good attorney would play them to keep Goldsby's name out of the paper and allow his client to walk free, although Deon would probably need a new profession.

"Hang tight, Deon," said Max.

Max and Joy stepped into the hallway.

Joy commented, "Funny, Grant corrupted Anne, and Anne, in essence, corrupted Deon."

Max said, "You don't really think it's all built into our DNA, do you, like you said to Grant? Deon chose poorly. We have choices, Joy."

"Sure, we do, Max. But we also have genetic predispositions."

Max and Joy entered the interrogation room across the hall from Deon.

A-gamer had been brought in so many times, he sat back, arms folded, as if he simply needed to get through the next hour and go home, a free man. He yawned.

"So, A-gamer," said Max, sliding into the chair opposite him, "Anne diverted hospital drugs and brought them to you."

"I don't know nothin' about drugs," said A-gamer. "She just liked my company."

This time, Joy paced, hovering over A-gamer to increase his discomfort. "Not so much. She slapped you—pretty hard, I hear—when you tried to make a move on her."

A-gamer tilted his head at a cocky angle. "If I wanted her, I'd have her. She's a phony. Too full of herself—like you."

Max redirected the conversation. "You said, and I quote, 'First she got cold feet. Then the rest of her got real cold.' Sounds like a confession to me."

A-gamer squirmed. "Don't try to pin her murder on me! I'm sure she had plenty of people who wanted her dead." A-gamer leaned forward, like he was preparing to make a deal. "But

Chief Goldsby, he liked her. He had a reason to shut her up. He threatened me."

"Let's back up," said Max, needing to maintain control of the interrogation. "You loaned Anne money."

A-gamer leaned back and chose his words carefully. "A personal loan. That's not against the law. I felt sorry for the chick. Did her right."

"Or did her dead," accused Joy.

A-gamer snickered. "I have an alibi—I was with my boys the night someone offed her."

"Where?" asked Max.

"The Stinky Mule." A-gamer snickered. "Does your chief have an alibi?"

"Convenient," argued Max. "No public witnesses—just you and your boys."

A-gamer didn't take the bait. Instead, he spoke with confidence, like he had his story all figured out and had just waited for the right time to deliver it. "You know, Goldsby was on the take. Wanted protection money. That's what I'll say when I testify. I'll fry his ass."

Max shot forward so hard and fast, it wiped the cocky grin off of A-gamer's face. "Well, Rice. That is your real name, right? Rice?"

"As in white rice?" asked Joy, sliding into the seat beside Max, ready to move in for the kill. "That's weak."

Max's voice rose higher with each word spoken. "Can you prove what you say about Goldsby? Because if you lie, I'll personally slam your cell door shut and pay regular visits to remind you what it costs to lie to us! So think carefully before you say another word." Max let that sink in.

Joy matched Max's energy. "We have a witness to your conversation with Anne and Goldsby—Deon. He'll testify that the chief closed Anne's account. That's all he did. Goldsby didn't make an exchange with you or anyone else, but Anne handed you a package. Anne stole drugs. Deon took over her route when Anne quit."

A-gamer stretched his arms. "Blondie repaid her loan—with cash. You can't prove otherwise. And I was with my crew when she died. You're wasting my time."

"Did Shane Drake bring you drugs from the pharmacy?" Max slid a picture from a folder and set it before A-gamer. "This guy."

A-gamer squirmed. He pushed the picture away. "What, now you want to pin two murders on me, plus whatever crimes this guy has done?"

Max scoffed, "Considering you just lied to us about Goldsby working for you—it's hard to believe a word you say."

A-gamer snapped. "I ain't no killer! Blondie needed money to feed her habit. She probably blackmailed Goldsby, and when he killed her, she squawked about this dude and the cop did him too. We're done here. I want a lawyer!"

Max rose to his feet. "You give one peep of false testimony, one fact you can't back up, and I do not mean back up with a bunch of lies from your mangy crew, and I promise you that my partner and I will see to it that your lily-white ass ends up in prison on a cell block with the biggest, baddest, most dangerous cons in the prison. Deon will cut a deal. He'll testify against you. He's got something you don't—credibility."

A-gamer fumed but kept silent, saving it for his legal defense.

Max opened the door. He and Joy stepped into the hallway.

Max fumed too. "Wall has a lot to lose. Let's get his story."

Max strutted into the interrogation room beside A-gamer's room. Joy followed.

For a big guy, Wall suddenly seemed like a little kid.

Max and Joy sat opposite him. He'd already been mirandized.

Max placed the two evidence bags in front of Wall. After

stating his legal name for the record, he said, "You were holding the drugs."

Wall didn't respond.

Joy said, "We already know about the altercation between A-gamer, Anne Martin, and Frank Goldsby. Deon will testify. What can you offer us that can keep you out of prison or keep you there for a shorter time?"

Wall sheepishly muttered, "Deon's a liar."

Joy said, "He's a witness." She placed pictures of Anne's and Shane's faces on the table. No corpse ever looked good in death, even pretty Anne Martin.

Wall's eyes grew wide. "This guy was a buyer. Opioids." He pointed to Shane Drake.

"Shane Drake? How often?" asked Max.

Wall shrugged, "Once a month, sometimes more. About a month ago, Deon dropped off his first package. This guy was there, buying. They met. They didn't know each other, so no big deal."

Max said, "For the record, you're saying Deon previously met Shane Drake at The Stinky Mule?"

"Right." Wall nodded. "Then, the night the blonde girl was killed, Deon stormed into the bar. He was frantic. Said he'd been to a poker game with the chief of police and a buyer recognized him. Deon was scared they guy would tell Anne about his dealing drugs to A-gamer."

Max asked, "What time did Deon get there?"

Wall pondered a moment. "Maybe eleven. He didn't stay long."

Joy asked, "What did A-gamer say to him?"

Wall crossed his arms over his chest, like imitating A-gamer's attitude. "He told Deon not to be so stupid. He said Anne had been stealing drugs too, and she wasn't going to incriminate herself, and the buyer had a habit, so he wouldn't be talking to anybody. And the chief was an idiot."

"How did Deon react?" asked Max.

Wall said, "He calmed down. A-gamer bought him a couple of shots of tequila. But, like I said, he didn't stay. He left."

Joy asked, "What time did he leave?"

"Maybe eleven-thirty," said Wall.

"Wait here. We're not done yet," said Max.

Max and Joy rose to their feet, shot out the door, and crossed the hall, entering Deon's room.

Max intentionally let the chair grate against the concrete as he pulled it out and sat down. Joy sat beside him.

Joy said, "You lied to us, Deon. You recognized Shane at the poker game. You saw him before at The Stinky Mule when you dropped off a supply, and he made a purchase."

Deon's eyes grew wide. "Which gives me an alibi! I was at The Stinky Mule the night Anne died. I told you I left the game early and went for a drink."

Max accused, "But you left the bar around eleven-thirty, which gave you plenty of time to get back to Eugene's house. Or did you go to Anne Martin's house first? Did you knock and she wasn't there? Did you come across her on the trail walking home? Did Dr. Grant knock her out and you smashed a rock against her skull to finish the job?"

Deon's eyes could not have grown any larger. He threw up his hands to stop the onslaught. "No way! I didn't kill Anne! I didn't kill anyone!"

Joy pressed him, "Shane was easy. Already an addict. You just had to wait for him, and when you found him napping, you stuck the Fentanyl patches on his back along with a heating pad. Problem solved."

Deon spoke so fast, he spit. "Stop it! You're making it up. I didn't do that! None of it!"

Max didn't stop. "But you needed a fall guy. You saw Goldsby confront A-gamer. It must have been funny when you discovered he was the chief of police?"

Joy added, "A perfect fall guy. He left his cigar clipper on the table. The patio door was open. You grabbed it and the cigar butt while Eugene had sex with Anne.'

"What? No! I want a lawyer. I'm not saying another word." Deon breathed hard. His shoulders rose and fell.

Joy shook her head. "It looks like student loans is the least of your worries."

Max stormed out the door, down the hall, and back to his desk. He fell into his chair.

Joy sat down in the chair beside him. It had become her work spot.

Max shook his head. "I know the evidence against the chief is circumstantial, but a good attorney will pit Goldsby against Deon against Dr. Grant. We'll never get a conviction."

"Max, we'll figure this out. I admit. It looks bad, but anyone at that game had access to the chief's cigar-cutter and cigar butt."

Max leaned on his elbows and dropped his weary head into his hands. "Some detective. Dad, I could use some help here." Max opened his eyes and saw a new report on his desk. He opened the folder and read it. His eyes lit up.

"Max? What is it?" asked Joy.

"There were two saliva samples on the cigar butt. The chief's and Eugene's."

"Eugene?" asked Joy.

"Maybe Eugene thought Anne had used him, so he followed her and lost control. He'd been dumped before. He couldn't take it again. It was a crime of passion. But why Shane?"

Joy said, "The doll house, Max. Cynthia was going marry Shane. Eugene wanted his daughter to dote on him and him alone."

"They do seem awfully close." Max pondered the idea. "Let's bring Eugene in for questioning. Now!"

24

By the time Max and Joy reached Eugene's house, the sun had been down about an hour. No one answered.

"Let's try the mortuary," said Max.

Max and Joy arrived in no time. They walked around back as they'd done before and entered the building.

Cynthia withdrew a plastic-wrapped leg from the freezer and passed it to her father, who set it gently in a cold-ship box. This time, they didn't flinch or stop working when Max and Joy strolled in.

The hair on Max's arms tingled as he watched the pair packaging body parts like one would pack a cooler for a picnic. Cynthia handed a head to her father, and he set it in the box with the same mannerisms he'd sipped his tea that morning.

"Eugene," said Max. "We're bringing you in for questioning."

At this, Eugene stopped working, huffed, and rolled his eyes. "Why? I'm innocent."

Joy answered. "We found your DNA on the cigar butt at Shane's house. It puts you there."

Eugene's brows rose into arches of terror.

Cynthia froze. "Papa?"

Max urged Eugene. "You need to come with us."

"There's been a mistake," said Eugene.

Cynthia rushed to her father and locked her arm through his. "Chief Goldsby is framing my father! This is how you police operate. Protect your own!"

Joy set her phone on the counter and said calmly, "Cynthia, your father needs to go. But I'll tell you what. I'll stay and help you with the order. Max, pick me up when you're done."

"Are you sure?" asked Max.

Joy nodded. "Eugene is right. There's no reason their business should suffer. I'll help Cynthia. "

"After you," said Max, holding out a pair of handcuffs. "Sorry, it's procedure."

Eugene allowed Max to cuff him. "I'll sue you. Both of you. The chief. The entire department. Hell, I'll sue the city!"

"Yeah, we hear that a lot, but you can't sue us for doing our jobs." Max led Eugene out the back door.

"What's the order?" asked Joy, moving beside the freezer as Cynthia took over packaging.

Cynthia answered matter-of-factly. "Four arms, four legs, two torsos, two heads. Hand me a leg. We try to ship specimens from the same body if possible. Look for Terence Cork."

Joy handed Cynthia a leg from the cooler. Joy thought back to her days of collecting dead creatures. In essence, beach goers picked up exoskeletons of dead organisms, fascinated by their beauty. Joy had studied death and the dead for so long, she felt more fascination than revulsion. The man and his soul had parted ways. The leg was akin to the dead shell on the beach— but not nearly as pretty. To deflect Cynthia's hostilities, Joy inquired about their business. "Any of these ever end up overseas?"

"We only ship within the US but other brokers ship overseas. If we get a request, we forward it to a larger tissue bank."

As Joy reached into the freezer and pulled out a skull to pass to Cynthia, she cringed at how Cynthia had used the stock-in-trade lingo "tissue bank" to normalize the fact that she held Terence Cork's head in her hands. She stared into the plastic-wrapped face and wondered, *Did you think this was where you would end up, Terence?* "Two arms and legs, we can match. Can't match two heads."

"Of course not," snapped Cynthia. "Now, I need two arms."

Joy handed Cynthia the head and searched the labels to find the arms. The body parts reminded her of her youth. Sam had brought home two dolls: an African Barbie and a Disney Perfume Princess. They didn't look like her. They wore shiny clothes and had lipstick-smiles.

Joy dismembered them and put their legs or arms on backwards. She popped their heads off and transplanted them onto the other body. She snipped their hair and gelled it into a mangled mess, used pens to give their faces and arms and legs character—like scars with large stitch marks—and she used a roll of black electrical tape she'd found in the garage to clothe them like some kind of steampunk soldiers. When satisfied, she sat them on the shelf and never played with them again. At least, they looked like how she felt. They belonged in her world. "I know of some countries that must have religious prohibitions or other restrictions for using their own dead for scientific purposes."

"You're right. Many countries do not allow this business, but they readily purchase tissue from the US to train their doctors or medical students or for research."

Joy found a matching arm and wished, momentarily, she

could put this person back together. She passed the arm to Cynthia.

Max sat across from Eugene in an interrogation room. Eugene hadn't said a single word in the car. And his demeanor had changed from outraged too subdued. Max hoped that meant he was ready to confess. Max mirandized him. "Do you understand your rights?"

"Of course I do," snapped Eugene. "I've nothing to hide." Eugene swallowed hard. "Let's get this over with. I need to get home."

Max informed Eugene he was being recorded and asked him to state his full name. He then asked, "How did your DNA end up on the cigar butt found at Shane Drake's house?"

Eugene's face drained of color, as if processing the revelation had drained every blood cell from his system all at once. "I don't know. The only cigar butt I smoked was the one the chief left in the ashtray. At the end of the evening, I...I saw it, and I took it. I slipped away to my room. I stepped out the French doors, stood on the patio, and I smoked it—two puffs, maybe three. Then I stubbed it out. I put it back before Cynthia cleaned up. She was busy with the glasses when I came back in the kitchen."

Max didn't like Eugene's answer or his bumbling presentation. "The chief carries more than one cigar. I'm sure he's offered you one before. What guy takes another guy's cigar and takes a couple of puffs?"

Eugene blurted, "Cynthia would have had my head! She doesn't like smoking or drinking. Her mother did both."

Max closed in. "The facts are that you were the last person to see Anne alive, Eugene—by your own admission—never mind the DNA you left behind. Was Anne drunk? Did she sleep with you and regret it?"

Eugene huffed, "Just because love didn't work out for me, it doesn't mean I killed anyone. Or that Anne used me. We made love. We made plans."

Max changed course to a more personal approach, hoping to open Eugene up to tougher questions down the road. "What happened to Cynthia's mother?"

Eugene's shoulders fell, like the memories of the past weighted them down. "She suffered from postpartum depression and started drinking."

Max scowled, "Maybe you depressed her, Eugene. She drank to escape from you?"

To Max's surprise, Eugene didn't balk. He agreed. "Maybe you're right. Linda was only seventeen when I got her pregnant. Our parents rushed us through a quick civil ceremony. Linda was eighteen when she had Cynthia. Not that age matters—but neither of us was ready for a family. I hid Linda's drinking. I didn't know about postpartum depression. I could have—I should have..." Eugene paused and closed his eyes momentarily. "By the time Cynthia was in her teens, it was bad. Cynthia would come home from school and find her mother passed out. She'd clean up vomit, cook dinner, and put her mother to bed. She never complained. Then the day came when Cynthia came home and found her mother floating in the pool. Frantic, she called me. That was when we lived in the old house. Linda had fallen, hit her head, and drowned."

"And Mayleen?" asked Max.

Eugene's cheeks sagged as he spoke. "Mayleen had problems. I thought she was past them. She said she loved me. We'd planned a vacation together. Hawaii. But, she left a note, took off, and I never saw her again."

"That must have pushed old buttons," said Max. "Maybe Anne came back to talk, to unload her problems, and you made a pass. She rejected you, so you followed her. You'd had enough of rejection. Grant admitted to striking her, but you finished the job. And you dropped the Chief's cigar cutter to cast the blame elsewhere."

Eugene's face turned ash-white. His brows pinched like Max hadn't seen before, like he drowned in his own thoughts and hadn't heard a word Max had said. "Cynthia is right. You protect your own. The chief is your man. His DNA was on that cigar. Goldsby is your man or Grant! They took the cigar butt. Or that loan shark that Shane mentioned. You leave Cynthia out of this!"

Max worked to understand Eugene's sudden shift in perspective and anger. Max reminded him, "Anne didn't deserve to die, Eugene."

Eugene leaned back. His voice had a finality to it. "No, she didn't. I'm guilty. Arrest me. Just let me talk to Cynthia."

Max's brain fired on all cylinders to process Eugene's sudden confession. Despite the fact he'd worked to get it, he hadn't expected it. Max churned ideas as they flew at him. He formed connections and reviewed scenarios. He thought out loud, but the words were barely audible. Max nearly whispered as he strung the bones together and layered on the flesh. "Cynthia. She found her mother dead. She didn't like Mayleen. She didn't approve of Anne."

Eugene leaned forward. "Mayleen had a troubled past. Drugs. Booze. She ran away, back to the fast life. And Anne—Grant is more than capable of killing her. If he couldn't have her, no one could. And...and Goldsby—that windbag—it was his cigar! His DNA."

Max leaned forward. He bore into Eugene's eyes. "Eugene—Cynthia needs help, just like Linda did."

Eugene looked down at his hands. His voice cracked, "Cynthia loved her mother. She cared for Linda. And for me. Cynthia knew her mother suffered from depression. I'm...I'm the guilty one. I didn't get Linda the help she needed. It's all my fault."

Max kept his voice low and steady. "Sending a man to prison for a crime he didn't commit won't help her." Max didn't wait another second. He had the answer. He bolted from the room and shouted to Steele as he ran past him, "Hold him! And send back-up to the mortuary! It's Cynthia. And Joy is with her."

Max raced to the parking structure and sank into the driver's seat of his car. He fired up the engine and turned on the siren and the lights. All Max could think of was his own guilt for having pushed Joy away. Eugene had ignored his wife's pain and Cynthia's, just like Max had ignored Joy's pain of separation. Joy spoke the truth. He was grounded, and he didn't care that she wasn't. What if he lost her?

The sirens screamed and the lights flashed in a new way—like a tornado warning that threatened to pluck Joy out of his life forever. Max shot into the night, "Hold on there, partner."

25

J oy handed Cynthia the last arm and watched her meticulously set it in the cooler, nudging this piece and that one like a human puzzle until it all fit together exactly right. "Anne liked your father very much."

Cynthia put on gloves and grabbed frozen gel packs from another freezer. She set them atop the body parts like packing steaks. "Anne liked many men. She didn't deserve a man as good as my father."

"Tell me about your mother."

"To be blunt, my mother was a drunk. Before I started to help out at the mortuary, I could protect my father. I'd put my mother to bed, so that by the time Papa got home, we had a peaceful, quiet dinner."

"You cared for your mother and your father. When did you start to cook?" asked Joy.

"I always helped mother in the kitchen. Otherwise, she'd burn things. By the time I was ten, I could make simple dishes —like spaghetti. Papa always raved about it. But by twelve, I'd started to find real recipes, like lasagna, and I'd surprise him. I love to cook."

"When did you start working here?" asked Joy, keeping her voice as soothing as a lullaby.

"After Papa and Kenneth started the tissue bank, father started coming home late, so I insisted that I help him after school to spend more time together. He let me, and while they worked, Papa, and sometimes Grant, would help me with homework." Cynthia set the last gel pack in place.

Joy asked, "How old were you?"

"Almost sixteen."

Joy asked, "And your mother? She must have spiraled without you to take care of her."

Cynthia moved between the freezer and the shipping container. She set a layer of dry ice over the gel packs. "Papa and I would come home and find mother passed out on the couch."

"I don't remember my mother," said Joy. "Just snippets. I wasn't even four when she died."

Cynthia stopped working and stared at Joy with a blank expression. "You're lucky. I came home from school one day and found my mother drowned in our pool."

Joy shifted her line of questioning. "Your father taking an interest in Mayleen, an ex party girl must have been frightful for you?"

Cynthia set a layer of bubble wrap over the dry ice, set the lid in place, and began to run packaging tape over the seam. "She wanted my father's money."

Joy closed the freezer. "You take care of your father. You protect him. You've always protected him. Did you kill you mother, Cynthia?"

Cynthia laughed lightly, as if Joy had told her about a smudge of flour on her cheek instead of murder. "My mother hit her head and fell into the pool."

"That's when you moved. Your dad built the house. I imagine he included you in picking out every detail."

"I like flowers."

Joy sensed a disconnect in Cynthia. It was like watching an emotionless automaton. "You took your mother's place, Cynthia. You gave yourself away with the doll house."

Cynthia kept taping the freezer box, but she eyed Joy like prey to be shredded and destroyed.

Joy elaborated, "No nursery. No children. Just a mother and a father—or a father and a daughter. The perfect house. But Mayleen moved in on your father. The first kill, your mother, that was probably unplanned, spur of the moment. Maybe you came home early and found her passed out by the pool. She just needed a nudge."

Cynthia ran tape over the edges of the container.

Joy continued, "Mayleen also required quick thinking. You probably lured her here with some pretense and lured your father away. Maybe he was busy packing for their trip. You killed Anne out of pure rage. You'd watched her flirt shamelessly. Your bedroom is just across the hall from your father's. You heard them. You waited until Anne left. You followed her. You saw her fight with Dr. Grant. He struck her in the jaw and stumbled away, drunk. You smashed a rock against Anne's skull and dragged her to the creek. You shoved her face into the mud. Problem solved. But Shane wouldn't let up—another addict in your life."

Cynthia stopped taping. She walked away from Joy and over to the stainless steel workbench. "The chief killed Anne and Shane."

Joy brought her scenario to a close with a gut-punch. "At some point, your father smoked that cigar. You cleaned up. You wanted to frame the chief, so you took his cigar cutter and the cigar butt, but you unwittingly framed your father instead of the chief." Joy set a hand on the freezer. "Did you keep a trophy? Is Mayleene in here—a piece of her anyway?"

Cynthia reached for the bone saw and flipped the switch.

The blade whined and whirred. "You're ruining everything!" She lunged, swinging the blade at Joy.

Joy leaped backward, striking her spine against the counter which halted her retreat. She had no where to go.

Joy grabbed Cynthia's forearm and tried to shove the blade away, but Cynthia redoubled her fierce and determined strength.

The whirling saw blade hovered a half inch away from Joy's cheek.

Joy gasped in disbelief a second before exulting a defiant grunt and defensively pushing the blade away inch-by-inch.

Cynthia grimaced as she applied added pressure. Her face twisted like a crazed Stepford robot bent on blood. Her eyes narrowed. Her teeth clenched. The muscles in her cheeks twitched with the effort.

The blade slid down until it hovered just above Joy's neck. Joy grimaced. She had to break the hold.

With one movement, Joy rammed her knee into Cynthia's pelvic bone and shoved the blade away.

The blade crashed down and bit into a steel table. Sparks flew.

Joy spun away to safety, her chest heaving. Her phone rang. She saw Max's name on her screen. She had no time to answer. "You wanted your father all to yourself, so you killed Shane."

Cynthia laughed. "He expected me to take care of him, and he'd take over working with Papa, so I could stay home and cook."

Suddenly, Joy saw Cynthia's tragic fight. "Your father chooses weak people. Addicts. Your mother, Shane, Mayleen, Anne. And Dr. Grant is his partner. You had to protect him."

"I will always protect him." Cynthia lunged forward with the saw.

Joy raced around a table and shoved it into Cynthia.

Cynthia caught the table, stopping its forward momentum.

Sirens blared in the distance.

Joy urged, "They're coming, Cynthia. They're coming for you. Put down the saw. I'll help you."

Cynthia shoved the table out of the way. It smashed against the freezer with a bang. Nothing stood between Cynthia and Joy. Cynthia raised the saw in the air, grimaced, and ran forward.

Joy threw up her hands to defend herself. Her sparring instincts emerged. She spun and kicked.

Cynthia grunted and swung the blade at Joy's leg as Joy's foot hit its mark and rammed into Cynthia's stomach.

The blade cut through Joy's pant leg and nicked her flesh. Joy grimaced as Cynthia flew backward and slammed into a wall.

Joy recovered quickly and realized that she was trapped in the corner. She curled her fists, ready to fight or lose a limb trying. Joy set her arms and legs into a sparring stance, ready to kick—it was the only option to keep Cynthia at a distance.

Cynthia lunged, aiming the saw at Joy's head.

A shot rang out.

Cynthia spun around and faced Max, who had fired a warning shot into the ceiling. Cynthia pressed the trigger of the saw and ran straight at Max.

"Shoot!" yelled Joy, somehow knowing that Max hesitated because she was in the line of fire.

In a split second, Max took aim and fired.

A red blotch grew at the corner of Cynthia's white apron, near her shoulder. Her arms fell to her sides. The saw slipped from her hands. The moment she released the trigger, the blade stopped spinning. The saw smacked the floor.

Joy rushed to Cynthia's side, knelt down, and pressed her hands over the wound. "Help is on the way, Cynthia."

Max dropped down beside them.

Steele stormed in behind Max. Behind him, other officers

filed in. "Call for an ambulance," shouted Max.

Steele shouted. "I already did. Just in case." He eyed Joy.

Joy heaved to catch her breath and nodded her thanks.

Steele shouted to others just outside. "All clear!"

An ambulance team flew into the room and started working on Cynthia.

Joy stood up.

Max put a hand on her shoulder. "Are you okay?"

Joy huffed. "I've still got four limbs. I thought you'd be here ten minutes ago."

"I'm the slow one, remember. You're the genius. No, I take that back. You put yourself in danger. Next time, *we* interrogate the suspects! You hear me?"

"It was a hunch, Max. I didn't know for sure. I had money on Eugene too. And Grant. And Golsby. And Deon. I needed to get Cynthia to open up. I'll bet Mayleen's is in the freezer. I'm sure of it. A piece of her, anyway. Cynthia would have kept a trophy. I'll bet there's a lock of her mother's hair somewhere in that dollhouse, too. Maybe in the chest in the attic."

Max let up. Like Joy said—she still had all her limbs—and Max still had her. He shook his head in jest, "Still a betting woman, I see. Let's get you out of here."

Max led Joy out of the room and across the gravel parking lot to the car. He opened the door for her, despite the fact she had no injuries and could have opened it herself, and Joy let him.

Max walked around the car and hopped in the driver's seat.

Joy was still catching her breath. "Maybe you should call the chief on the way back. Let him know he's in the clear."

"Hmmm. That would be the right thing to do." Max's voice had a tinge of sarcastic devilry.

Joy added, "Of course, you have a report to file first. That could take some time. Hours."

Max dipped his chin in agreement. "That it could, pardner."

26

The following morning, Chief Frank Goldsby strutted into the station like a man who had walked through a blazing fire and stepped out unscathed. He paraded through the station as if taking a victory lap. He nodded as he passed by officers instead of his norm of beelining a path to his office with as little interaction as possible. He even said "good morning" a few times.

His strut lacked humility. If anything, the experience had bloated his confidence.

The chief pulled Max and Joy into his office and closed the door. He sank into his seat as if reclaiming a lost parcel of land. He leaned forward and folded his hands to set a stake in the dirt. His eyes still had dark circles from too much Merlot, too many cigars, and too little sleep, but his cheeks flushed with color again, intensifying the tiny spider veins and broken capillaries. "Joy, I'd like to extend your contract indefinitely. Hire you, in fact. Since you completed FBI training and worked for the San Diego PD, it's an easy transfer. Your expertise led to an arrest in this case."

Joy immediately rushed to correct him. "Thank you, Chief Goldsby, but I didn't solve this case. Max led the team."

Goldsby eyed Max. "I can offer you a partner with more experience. Max is green."

Max's shoulders stiffened. He'd become the invisible man in the room—no, the invisible elephant. Maybe the chief had a point—he was an idiot. What did he expect? That Goldsby would slap a gold star on his forehead and say "attaboy"? The chief didn't roll that way. Ever. Not when it came to him. "May I be excused, chief? I've got a job to do—and I'm damn good at it. You know it. I know it. And as far as I'm concerned, the latter is the more important of the two."

Goldsby ignored his request and added a dig. "Am I right, Max? Don't you think Dr. Burton is an asset to the force?"

"Of course I do," said Max.

Joy threw her shoulders back, ready to fight. "I appreciate that you think I've got brains, because I do. And it's for that reason that I'm telling you that Max has natural instincts. And *that*, chief, is equally if not more important than brains. His gut and his head cracked this case. If not for Max, you'd be playing in the sandbox with Pokey and the gang in prison."

"Am I dismissed?" Max gritted his teeth and waited.

Joy leaned in even farther, not in defeat, but as a gesture to move into the chief's space. "Excuse Max and I'll give you my answer."

Something about Joy's expression undermined Goldsby's confidence. He leaned back. "You're excused, Detective King."

Max returned to his desk.

In short order, Joy approached with the chief beside her.

Goldsby's face burned crimson red. The veins on his neck bulged as he barked orders, "Find Dr. Burton a desk!" He didn't wait. He disappeared with his tail between his legs.

Reed Steele and another officer grabbed a vacant desk and

hauled it over to Max's station. They placed the desk edge-to-edge with Max's, such that he and Joy faced one another.

Steele grabbed a chair, and Joy sat down in it. Steele whispered, "I'm feeling crazier by the minute, doctor. How 'bout a drink after work?"

"Seven. My place," said Joy matter-of-factly. "If Monty likes you, you can stay."

"Did Monty like me?" asked Max.

Joy replied, "She crawled over to greet you, didn't she?"

Steele's brows knitted in confusion, as he struggled to ascertain if Monty was a child, a pet, or something else.

Max helped him out. "Don't worry, Steele. Monty is twenty-one."

Steele's face made a quick, "ah," of relief, since it clarified that Monty was not a small child, but then his brows furrowed with new assumptions as he tried to pair "crawled" with the age. An old, old dog or cat came to mind. "Great, I'll catch you later. Welcome to the Wine Valley PD, Joy." Steele walked away scratching his head.

Joy gazed at Max. "Hey, pardner."

Max suggested, "You should ask Steele to the Wolf's dinner party on Friday."

"First, the Monty test. Second, my test. And, if he passes, maybe the dinner party."

Max contemplated the kind of psychological test a forensic psychologist would put a date through. On the other hand, he had a habit of leaving the detective work at the station—a bigger mistake. In social settings, he let down his guard. But that had often cost him a relationship and hurt feelings. When he met Susan, the last girl he had dated, he stepped into the relationship with a let's-just-have-some-fun-and-see-how-it-goes mentality. He thought she had done the same.

Susan, a pretty blond personal trainer, never came out and

said, "I want to get married and have your babies," but it became evident through her choices of social engagements. He booked concerts, movie nights, wine tastings, hot air balloon rides, and plenty of Western dancing at Sal's Saloon—and she booked backyard barbecues at the homes of married friends with children, or family events, at which time she'd drop hints, like "What adorable children. I can't wait to have my own."

Max never picked up on hints, since he somehow didn't really think they related to him. He took them as her expression of *her* future desires, which he thought pretty cool, but that was not the case. She expressed her future desires with *him*.

Max figured it out three months in when Susan asked for his key, as in the key to his apartment—he only moved back to the hacienda after his father died. Susan wanted to make dinner for Max. He freaked out, which led to Susan freaking out and shouting, "It's not like I'm asking to live together!" Then he realized she missed clues too. A key—everyone knows—is synonymous with "my space is your space" and a hop-skip-and-jump from "let's live together." It's a total departure from "but aren't we just hanging out and having fun?"

To Max's relief, Susan stormed out of his life in a huff after calling him "immature." But Joy—the genius raised by an FBI profiler—must have psychological, physical, mental, and emotional tests never encountered by man before. As Max began to consider what those various tests might be, he realized Joy was staring at him, as if waiting for him to say something. He blurted, "Does this mean you're quitting your night job?"

One side of Joy's mouth turned up in a half smile. "When the day comes that training law enforcement personnel to recognize the symptomatology and character traits of demented killers is no longer needed, I'll pack up my podium. So, no, Max. No dodging your homework. I expect you in your seat Monday night."

"I'm beginning to think that if I ever figure you out, Joy, I'll be a damn good detective."

"That's a great place to start." Joy pulled her laptop out of its case and set it on the desk.

Max could not pinpoint the mysterious feeling that pinched his gut like sonar on search and destroy mode when he looked at Joy. He desperately needed to turn that switch off, to stop searching. But it pinged again and again, pricked at him, and finally stabbed him so hard, he had to face it.

The signal was suddenly received and deciphered.

At the funeral, when he first encountered Joy, he wanted to confront her—to dig into her brain and extract her secrets—his secrets. But that all changed the moment he saw the note on the back of the picture where their adoptive fathers stood side-by-side. And yet, here was Joy, facing him.

Their eyes locked, and he knew he could not escape her, nor could he escape the beastly shadow that lurked behind her —the shadow of the past.

How would this work? Was this her plan? To infiltrate? To face him until he could no longer hide anymore? Was this his psychological test?

Max eyed the room, leaned forward and whispered, "What did you do to Goldsby? Blackmail him?"

Joy leaned in and whispered back. "Let's just say that the chief and I had a meeting of the minds. You have to know your enemies, Max. You have to get inside their head. I gave the chief what he wanted—me—and he gave me what I wanted—you."

"Remind me not to go head-to-head with you."

"I need you to go head-to-head with me, Max. I'm counting on it."

"Why?"

"To keep me sane."

Steele arrived at Joy's house just before sunset.

Joy opened the door wearing a low-cut simple black tank dress that hugged her slender frame, no shoes, and no bra.

Steele had dressed casually—jeans and a clean cotton shirt, but now he wished he'd have stuck to the more casual T-shirt. He worried that Joy would think he was trying too hard, which he was. The moment he laid eyes on her face, her dark eyes pulled him in. His heart did a dance inside his chest that he'd never felt before. But then, his life up until he moved to Wine Valley some months ago had been consumed by hunting down his brother's killer, the most notorious gang leader in LA, and nothing else.

Steele felt Joy's eyes on him as he stepped through the door. It felt like he had walked through an airport security scanner, and he suddenly felt self-conscious.

Joy tilted her head and gazed at every rolling muscle of his shoulders, and when he turned, he caught her raising her eyes off of his butt and giving him a little half smile of approval. *Man*, he thought to himself, *now I know how girls feel*.

"Do I call you Reed or Steele? Cops are picky that way. You get used to hearing your last name more than your first sometimes."

"Steele."

Joy led the way.

Yellow walls and white ceilings dominated every room but for accents of green in the dining room, red and yellow floral furniture in the living room, and navy blue in the kitchen. "Colorful," said Steele. "I like it."

"Sam, my adoptive father, decorated this house. He passed away in January. I inherited it."

"I'm sorry. About your dad, I mean." Steele commented, "You keep it toasty in here."

"Monty likes it warm."

Since Joy didn't offer any Monty details, Steele backpedaled. He didn't know what to say. The best his brain could muster was, "L.A. peaked at 117 last summer during a heat wave. I can handle heat." He kicked himself. It sounded so cliché or worse, like a sexual innuendo.

Joy slid open the French doors and stepped onto a slate patio. A ceiling fan in the patio cover rotated, sending gentle waves of air over them.

Steele settled into a gray wicker love seat with black cushions that faced a stone hearth where a fire blazed. The golden dusk didn't need a fire yet, but it would be nice when the sun fully set.

Joy asked, "Beer, whiskey, or wine. I've got a Burgundy opened."

Steele brushed his jeans, which didn't need brushing. He did it to settle his nerves. "Whiskey straight up would be great." Why did she unnerve him so?

Joy ducked inside.

Steele admired the view of the distant hills—golden but fragile, dry grass and tinder capable of igniting into a firestorm.

Joy returned and set a whiskey in Steele's hand and set a glass of wine down for herself. "Be right back."

"I'll be here." *Lame!* Steele scolded himself.

Joy returned with a platter of appetizers.

"Wow! I thought maybe I'd take you to dinner." Steele recognized the prosciutto and cheese, vegetables, kebob, and that was all. "This looks pretty fancy."

"Actually, it's as basic as a person can get." Joy settled next to Steele, pulled her legs up to the side, and slid her arm over the backrest of the love seat as if she needed it for extra support while she leaned forward to point out the samplings.

Steele caught himself checking out Joy's figure at the new angle. Leaning forward enhanced the firm mounds of her breasts. He chastised himself for enjoying the view, until Joy turned her head and grinned, obviously pleased that he had noticed.

"I'm going through a raw foods phase. So, there's salmon and tuna sashimi. And this is venison carpaccio, basically thinly sliced, pounded raw venison, sprinkled with olive oil, lemon, and topped with shaved white truffle."

"Where did you get the venison?"

Joy locked her black-brown eyes on Steele's hazel ones and used her Wednesday Addam's voice. "In the woods."

"I know, I mean—"

Joy laughed. "Just kidding, Steele. Sam started teaching me how to hunt when I was like seven."

Steele's face lit up. "I make awesome jerky. How about a trade?"

Joy smiled. "Deal. I'll give you some venison before you leave, if you promise to share some jerky with me. Do you hunt?"

"Just bad guys and gals."

Joy's nodded. "That's enough. And, in case you like your meat cooked there's kabab with veggies and dip."

"I like my steak bloody," said Steele. "Ever tried *kitfo*?"

"Never heard of it," said Joy.

"In L.A., I had an Ethiopian informant. He died." Steele felt like he'd opened a deep wound. He pressed on. "Abel's mother had me over for dinner before I left LA to thank me for trying to get her son out of a gang. She made me this spicy raw hamburger dish. Pretty good. She cooked stuff too."

"I'll have to look that up." Joy grabbed her glass. Steele did the same. Joy asked, "To new friends."

Steele clinked his glass with Joy's and took a big swig of whiskey. He was disappointed at the word "friends." He'd hoped for more. Way more. He reminded himself to slow down. After all, he hadn't had any meaningful relationships up to now

—girls didn't fit in with his former obsession to hunt down gang leader Enrique Otero.

Joy reached for a piece of carpaccio and playfully dangled it in front of Steele's mouth.

Steele playfully gobbled it up, licking Joy's fingers in the process.

Joy added, "I don't eat anything raw that hasn't been deep frozen to thirty below first. Just so you know."

"The rawer the better, Joy." Steele cringed. "That did not come out right." They both laughed.

As they ate, they kept to safe subjects like Steele's entry into the police force and Joy's pursuit of forensic psychology. They remained within the confines of the approved topics of conversation, warmed by the fire.

They refilled their drinks once more.

Joy finally said, "It's time to meet Monty."

"I admit, I'm curious," said Steele.

Joy led Steele inside, down the hallway, and into her bedroom.

Steele felt like he'd stepped into Africa. The room had cane furniture, red walls, a white ceiling, a black bedspread, and a black couch at the end of the bed with a white fur throw. On the walls, silver frames contained black and white prints of predator animals in the heat of the hunt.

"Dad's décor?" asked Steele.

"No! Sam liked sunny yellow. I can't sleep in yellow. This is the only room I've redone."

Steele wondered why she called her father Sam, but he let it go.

Joy stepped toward a custom-built black reptile cabinet, half a dozen feet tall. It ran the length of the back wall, stopping short of the French patio doors, and jutted a few feet into the room.

Joy opened one of the cabinet doors. She stepped inside the

enclosure, which had terraced rock walls, logs and branches, green leafy plants, hideaways, and a shallow pool. She reached high to where a large snake basked on a branch. A lamp shone down on its thick coils of scaly mahogany-brown skin with light brown splotches rimmed in cream. It moved at a slow pace, reaching its head down toward Joy, as if to climb into her arms.

Joy orchestrated the lift to avoid injury. She stepped out of the enclosure and over to the bed.

Steele followed and sat on the edge of the mattress. The snake had to be five feet long and several inches thick.

Joy sat in the middle of the bedspread and coiled Monty in her lap. "This is Monty."

"Boa?"

"Ball python. Female."

"Monty Python—cute. Can I hold her?"

"Take off your shirt," said Joy.

While Steele liked Joy's command, he hesitated to read her meaning as anything but snake-related, although he hoped otherwise.

Joy cocked her head. "Monty likes the feel of skin best. Silk or satin is her next favorite. Cotton, not so much. She's spoiled."

Steele wasn't sure a python that crawled over leaves and trees in its enclosure really preferred silk to cotton, but he could see that Joy liked the feel of Monty's skin, as she continued to stroke her.

Steele shed his shirt, sat close to Joy, and crossed his legs.

Joy let out an involuntary gasp and ran her finger over a scar that began at the tip of Steele's sternum and ducked beneath the waistband of his jeans. She locked onto his eyes and held his gaze.

Steele felt like he looked into a mirror. That single look spoke volumes. Steele didn't know who Joy was yet, but he understood one thing about her—children either grew up in sunny yellow worlds or black shadowy ones. Children nurtured in the sun basked in the light, spread their arms, and peered skyward to gaze up at fluffy clouds and blue skies and the brilliant golden orb. They liked yellow.

But he and Joy had grown up in dark shadowy worlds with predators. Their eyes had been pulled down into the pit, forced to see what no child should see, and it forever changed them; it excluded them from the games played by the children of the light, who lacked the ability to see darkness. Darkness frightened them. But it was all he knew. Instinct told him that it was all Joy knew too. He'd watched his brother Dante—caught in gang crossfire at the age of ten—bleed out. What had Joy been through? He wanted to know, and he wanted to hold her while she told him.

Steele broke the silence. "The Ethiopian kid I told you about? I stopped a bullet meant for him. The doctors had to rip me open fast to stop the leaking."

"You saved his life."

"Not for long," said Steele. "While the doctors fixed the carnage, the gang leader tortured and killed Abel. He'd have been better off taking the bullet. Abel's mother came to see me in the hospital. She didn't blame me, but I did. I needed Abel to get inside the gang, so I could find the man who shot and killed my brother Dante when we were kids."

Joy leaned forward, kissed Steele's scar, and pulled back. "You can't see my scars. Well, except for this tiny one on my wrist. It's a scratch."

Steele gripped Joy's wrist. He rubbed the tiny scar with his thumb, brought it to his lips, and kissed it. "Oh, yeah, I see them." Steele felt a surge of warmth throughout his body. His heart raced. The temperature in the room felt like a second skin. He'd never felt so comfortable with anyone before—off-balance and out of his comfort zone in one way and perfectly in sync in another. Joy didn't need to say a word—neither of them did. She sucked in a deep breath, as if what he'd said had struck a chord.

Joy lifted Monty into the air, knelt on the bed, and draped Monty around Steele's neck and down his rippling stomach.

The sensation blew Steele's mind. To his surprise, having a five-foot long python around his neck seemed as natural as having Joy beside him. "She's beautiful."

Joy pulled free the band that kept Steele's hair in a tidy ponytail. She ran her fingers through his tresses. "I've wanted to do that from the moment we met." She added a nervous, "I'm glad you like Monty. Not everyone does."

"I like everything about you, Joy, and that includes Monty."

Monty turned her head and crept up Steele's chest.

Joy stroked Monty's head. "It was love at first sight at the pet store. Makes me a strange duck."

Monty flicked her pink tongue.

Steele stroked Monty's skin. "I'm a strange duck too."

Joy let out a sigh, like she'd waited a lifetime to meet one of her own kind. "Time for my girl to make an exit." Joy lifted Monty from Steele's shoulders, scooted off of the bed, set Monty back in her enclosure, and latched the door.

As Joy strolled back to Steele, she slipped her black dress off of her shoulders and let it fall to the ground. She wore nothing but black lace panties.

Steele's heart beat faster in his chest, watching Joy approach. He'd never seen any woman as beautiful or as terrifying. Why did she unnerve him? Did he unnerve her?

Joy crawled on the bed like an animal on the prowl. She reached for the top button on Steele's jeans.

Steele didn't resist. He let out a sound of pleasure, feeling her fingers curl and press against his abdomen. He reached out and gripped her hips firmly in his hands.

Joy had no sooner begun to unzip Steele's jeans than he lay back and shimmied out of his remaining clothes.

Joy did the same, letting out a breathless sigh that could have been a purr as she tossed her lace panties aside.

Joy straggled Steele. Her legs held him captive. She leaned down over him, and kissed him without any hesitation or reserve. The kiss was mutual. Hot, deep, demanding.

Joy's skin glimmered like warm honey against Steele's tawny chest and arms.

Steele had never had a first kiss as unintimidated and explorative—almost carnal. He reached his hands around Joy's waist and pulled her down on top of his chest.

Joy fell against him, willing to relinquish control, like a cliff-diver trusting the trajectory and beauty of the fall. She brushed her lips against Steele's neck, teasing, taunting.

Steele thrust his fingers through her hair and brought her lips to his. Steele whispered, "Maybe you'll like me more than Monty."

Joy whispered, "She has twenty-one years on you, Steele."

"I'll catch up." Steele kissed her, harder this time, like he wanted to share his world with her all at once.

Like thirsty nomads who came upon a desert oasis, they drank each other in, thirsting more with each taste or touch.

They set reason aside and let instinct and sensation guide every movement. Until, in desperate longing, they merged.

Like coupling snakes, they writhed and twisted and constricted.

They feasted, filling their bellies until they stood at the brink of satisfaction that neither of them had ever felt before— the urgent need to belong to something greater than them-selves. It surpassed their ability to linger and tarry.

Like two dark flint stones striking against one another, sparks flew, ignited a flame, and burned through them, engulfing them.

The heat soared in tempest and temperature until a simul-taneous explosion rocked them to the core of their being.

As the shock waves subsided and their breathing slowed, they coiled their arms around one another.

Steele squeezed Joy's shoulders and kissed her head. "So, does Monty like me?"

Joy grinned and ran a hand over Steele's chest. "I think you're growing on her, Steele."

THE NEXT CASE

Friday night, the police station emptied quickly. Joy changed into a red and black silk dress that hugged her slender frame and accentuated the soft pillows of her breasts. Black crystal clips gently pulled her hair back behind her ears, and matching crystal earrings dangled from her earlobes, caught the light, and danced playfully.

Even in a dress, Max could picture Joy leaping Ninja-style and cutting someone's throat. Maybe he just needed to give her more credit, give her the benefit of the doubt that she had a soft side.

Per Max's directive to be dressy-casual, Steele wore a dark suit jacket, a white shirt, and jeans. He wore his hair pulled back and banded.

Max donned fancy cowboy attire: a black suit, black shirt, black Stetson, and his father's favorite silver bolo tie, a gift bestowed on David at a summer pow wow at the Golden Earth Casino. The silver motif at his neck could have been a wheel or a flower. Max didn't know. He had an impressive collection of his own bolo ties—some presents from his father, others bought on his own—but this tie kept his recently deceased father close by, and he needed that.

Max handed Joy the address to the Wolf's home and proceeded to fill Joy and Steele in on who'd they'd meet at the birthday party. It sounded like a briefing prior to setting out on patrol: "Joy, you can fill Steele in on Red and Kate. They have five sons, but Danny passed away a month ago, that's Lizzy's husband. She's the birthday girl. The other four sons—Liam, Logan, Jack, and Alfie—all work at the winery. Liam married Cathy, a former Miss Wine Valley pageant winner, about fifteen years or so his junior. Cathy did not make it past the local pageant, but she acts like there's still a tiara on her head. Logan married his life-partner, Matteo, a couple of years back at the winery. They met in Italy, when Logan studied abroad for a year. Big wedding. Jack is divorced. Alfie is close to may age and single. Lizzy hails from the Kinsey Pharmaceuticals empire, started by her father Harold Kinsey. And that is all you need to know, except that Sally, Lizzy's much older half-sister, will be there. According to Red and Kate—mostly Kate—Sally is a man-eating she-devil. She's CEO of Kinsey Pharmaceuticals and always on the prowl—even though married. I've seen her around town, but I've never actually met her, so I'm curious. My dad once said that Sally—and I quote—'registers somewhere between plumb-loco and plumb-ornery.'"

"I'm at home with plumb-loco," said Joy. "Should be fun."

Steele added, "And if plumb-ornery, means plumb-mean, then I can handle it."

Max drove his blue convertible through the open gate and up a winding road to the Wolf estate. Steele and Joy followed him in Steele's Jeep Wrangler, white with black trim. They parked on the paver-stone driveway, more like a modest parking lot, before a massive, two-story house with a stone façade. This was no castle. It was a Scottish manor house fit for royalty and built on a different corner of the vineyard than the winery and hotel.

They'd barely rung the sonorous bell, when Kate swung the door wide and waved them inside. Kate had tamed her wild red waves of hair by pulling them back with a black velvet hair ribbon. She wore a modest black dress and flat shoes. "So happy you made it. Welcome to our home."

"Thank you," said Joy. "This is Reed Steele."

Kate ushered her guests inside. "Come in. Come in."

"Lovely home," said Joy, her eyes roaming from warm wood beams or panels to lofty crown moldings to antiques on display.

A massive wooden staircase with a carpeted runner swooped up to the second level from the cobbled stone floor of the foyer. A central table with a stunning bouquet of flowers sat upon a round, lustrous carpet with intricate designs and rich colors. Paintings of highland landscapes, which looked like original masterpieces in gilt frames, adorned the walls. Max seemed right at home.

"Thank you, Joy. Welcome," said Red, entering the foyer and reaching out for a firm handshake with his guests. "Let's get you a *bevvy*."

"That'd be a drink," said Kate. "Been here decades, but we still talk like Scots."

Red led them into an elegant living room with a cathedral, white-paneled ceiling, a massive stone hearth, heavy wood furnishings, tapestry-like drapes, and picture windows that beheld rolling hills blanketed with rows of grapevines as far as the eye could see.

Red approached the bar, while Kate meandered outside to attend to the other guests, sitting at tables or standing along the patio balustrade while watching the sun set over the vineyard and the western hills.

Red said, "I uncorked a few bottles from the cellar—our award-winning Pinot Noir, Sauvignon Blanc—or I could make ye a Glasgow punch, a Scotch muffler, or might I suggest a half an' a half, which would be a small whiskey and a tall ale?"

"Pinot Noir, thank you," said Joy.

"Same," said Max.

"I gotta go with the half an' a half," said Steele, "as I suspect it's really good whiskey."

Red smoothed his beard. "'Tis one of the best. And a fine ale too. I'm 'avin' the same."

Drinks in hand, Max, Joy, and Steele followed Red outside. The golden-orbed sun sank toward the silhouette of hills that separated Wine Valley from the Pacific Ocean. The sky blossomed with color: blue above and ochre at the horizon.

Alfie, the youngest son, stood near the balustrade next to his older brother, Jack. Alfie was clean-shaven and freckle-faced. Jack sported a beard as thick as his father's. Both showed the family resemblance to their parents. "Hey, Max," said Alfie.

"I'll leave you young'uns to it," said Red, already sauntering over to Lizzy's table.

Max spotted Sally, and she spotted him, eyeing him like candy. Max turned away.

"Good to see you, Max." Jack's eyes roved over Joy as he waited for introductions.

Suddenly caring more about freeing up a hand and less about decorum, Steele tossed back his whiskey and set the shot glass on a nearby table, freeing up one hand to slide around Joy's waist.

Max said, "Joy Burton, my partner, and Reed Steele, my good friend."

Jack and Alfie shook hands with them.

"Come on," said Alfie, addressing Joy and Steele. "I'll introduce you to the others." He strolled over to a table occupied by three men and the former beauty queen. Cathy—a true beauty with a delicate nose, sky-blue eyes, and shoulder-length blond hair. Cathy waved and shot them a perky white-toothed smile, which bubbled with over-the-top, wide-eyed glee. She'd accentuated her tall, hour-glass figure by wearing a baby blue dress that clung to her ample breasts, tiny waist, and slender hips.

Alfie said, "This is Joy and Reed. Max, you know." He rattled off the names of the guests at the table for Joy and Steele.

Jack grabbed a chair and sat down to join his relatives.

Cathy gushed, "David King—your daddy—judged the Miss Wine Valley pageant I won. He had you in tow. Gosh, that had to be a decade ago."

Max laughed. "It was. I'd just turned sixteen. I felt like I'd landed in the kingdom of the Amazon women. My friends were totally jealous."

Cathy laughed. "Now this beautiful girl here could have won the whole shebang. Darlin', that is a show-stoppin' dress."

Before Joy could respond, Matteo interceded, "Cathy. Pause and breathe, dear." Matteo spoke with a mild Italian accent. He had dark, thick, wavy hair and fashionable stubble.

Liam and Logan laughed in stereo as brothers brought up together naturally did. It was clearly all in good humor, not to embarrass Cathy. Liam, the oldest brother and Cathy's husband, extended an invitation. "Join is if you dare."

Cathy shook her head. "Oh, yes, Joy. Please have a seat. I'm horribly outnumbered here."

Alfie intervened. "In a bit. I'm makin' the rounds first." Alfie strolled to the next table. Extra chairs had been squeezed in to make room for seven, and even then, Lizzy's boys stood nearby.

Lizzy jumped up to greet Max with a heartfelt hug. "Thanks for coming, Max. How have you been?"

Max hugged Lizzy back. In the past few weeks, they'd exchanged the unpleasantness of attending one another's family funerals: Danny's and David's. "Probably the same as you, Lizzy. I'm hanging in there. I miss dad. How's it going for you?"

"It goes. Day-by-day." Lizzy's face showed age and fatigue. She'd lost weight. Despite dressing up for her birthday, her thin shoulders sagged, and her blouse and slacks ballooned over bone-thin appendages. Her green eyes struggled to create a spark, and her mouth turned up in an obligatory smile. "These are my sons, Rio and Oliver. Rio just finished his bachelors in biochemistry at UCLA and came on board with Kinsey."

Rio quickly interjected, "For a while, mom." He turned to the guests, "Then it's on to grad school."

Max could feel the palpable tension. Clearly, Rio had put his academics on hold to care for his ailing father, but now that Danny had passed, he could resume his studies. Lizzy had adopted Rio when he was four years old, and then became pregnant with Oliver, who had her features and Danny's red hair. Rio had olive skin and dark hair and eyes.

Joy asked, "Have a favorite?"

Rio didn't hesitate, "Cal Tech."

Joy nodded her approval.

Max introduced his friends. "This is Joy Burton and Reed Steele, colleagues."

Lizzy countered with introductions of the others at her table. "This is my sister, Sally, and her husband Elliot. I don't think you've ever met them before."

Max noticed the stark difference between the two sisters. Sally had to be in her fifties, but she exuded fire and sexuality and something else, maybe ruthlessness. Her garnet-red hair, spiked this way and that, her red lips and thick, black mascara gave her a witch-like appearance—a cruel beauty. Elliot, her husband, was a balding, slim man with glasses, who exuded no emotion whatsoever.

Despite drooping eyelids, one lower than the other, Sally's

hickory-brown eyes swept up and down Joy briefly, before locking onto Max like a bear to honey. "Nice to meet you."

As if fully aware of Sally's appetites, Alfie added, "Sally, these folks are part of our wonderful Wine Valley's police force."

Sally grinned. "I like policemen." Sally slurred as if already inebriated. No one laughed.

Lizzy shot Max an apologetic look.

With the sweep of her hand and dragon-red nails, Sally introduced the last two at the table. "This is Todd Barr, my fabulous attorney, and Alice Worth, my mediocre assistant." Sally laughed at her own joke, but no one else laughed with her. Sally quickly added. "I'm just joking, people. Alice, you're fabulous too." Her tone was less than sincere.

Todd, about Sally's age and with salt-and-pepper hair and wire-rimmed glasses, reached over and squeezed Alice's hand, but he quickly let go. The young assistant had hazel eyes and chestnut hair pulled back in a ponytail. She wore a gray pantsuit over a pin-striped blouse that gave her a masculine look, yet if she let her hair down, she'd be quite attractive.

A devilish grin crossed Elliot's face. "She's lasted two whole months working for you, dear. Don't blow it now."

On that sour note, Kate rose to her feet. "Max, Reed, Joy—take our seats. Red and I have to check on the kitchen staff. Sally, Elliot, thanks for sending Maria over to help out."

Sally nodded. "Of course, she's happy to make some extra cash."

As Red grabbed his pint and his whiskey and rose to his feet, he had the happy expression of a man who'd been saved.

Sally shifted her weight and rubbed her stomach.

"Are you all right?" asked Todd.

"Not sure," said Sally, still slurring. "Upset stomach."

Oliver reached over and grabbed Sally's empty wine glass. "I'll get you some water, Aunt Sally."

"Wine," ordered Sally.

Alice rose to leave. "And I need to get back to work and help out, so you will all have a fabulous dinner." Alice said the word fabulous with Sally's intonation.

"Guys, let's put these tables together," said Jack, already rising to his feet and gripping the table edge. Matteo and Liam assisted. They scooted the table over, and all resumed their seats, having formed one large group.

Oliver returned and set a glass of Pinot Noir in front of Sally. She didn't say a word of thanks. She just grabbed the glass and swigged, keeping an eye on Max the entire time.

Cathy broke the silence. "Joy, you're a police woman too? What made you choose such a dangerous job? At the sight of blood or a gun, I'd surely faint. I'd be no help at all."

"I am what I am, Cathy. The job chose me. I joined the force as a consultant, but I'm on board full-time now," said Joy. "I'm a a forensic psychologist."

Sally roared with laughter and waved her dragon nails. "I'm sorry. It's just that I have this picture in my head of your analyzing a bank robber or maybe a shoplifter. He's stretched out on the couch." Her voice sank to a low, mocking tone. "You ask, 'What made you do it?'"

Joy kept her usual straight face and monotone voice. She tilted her head and bore her eyes into Sally's. She stepped forward like an animal closing the distance on a target. "My specialty is psychoanalyzing murderers, Sally. So if you ever kill anyone, I'd be the person sitting across from you, like now, and I'd peel you like an onion..." Joy set down her glass and held up a clawed hand that held an invisible onion. She motioned like she was peeling layer after layer, "until I reached the rotten core." Joy clenched her fist, squishing the invisible onion.

Sally's smile fell, while others restrained any slip of laughter but allowed for the slightest grin, a barely perceptible upturn at the corners of their mouths.

Sally rose from the table and wobbled on her feet. "Elliot, Todd, we're going inside."

Elliot picked up Sally's wine glass and took her by the arm. "Let's get you some water, dear." Todd tried to take her by the other arm. Sally ripped herself loose from them both and stormed ahead.

They'd no sooner left than Matteo wriggled in his seat and sank down, whispering, "I'm melting...I'm melting." The others quickly figured out the allusion to the bad witch in *The Wizard of Oz*.

Logan shushed him, nodding toward Lizzy.

Matteo said, "*Mi scuzi*, Lizzy. I know she's your sister."

Lizzy's face brightened, and a genuine smile crossed her lips. "She's my sister—not by choice. But you all, on the other hand, are my family. I don't know where I'd be if I hadn't have met Danny." She raised her glass. "To Danny."

Logan raised his glass. "To Danny. And happy birthday, Lizzy. From your family."

"Here, here," added Jack.

"We love you, Lizzy." Cathy held a hand over her heart and clinked her wine glass with Lizzy's. "Always."

Max, Steele, and Joy clinked glasses too, and the laughter grew as the sun set.

Not long after, Maria stepped outside and approached the tables. "Dinner is served."

Once inside, Joy strolled down the hallway to the bathroom. She spotted Oliver taking the top off of a small bottle. He titled his head back and held the bottle over his right eye.

Sally emerged from the bathroom, wobbly on her feet.

Plop. The drop splashed in Oliver's eye.

Sally brushed past them. She put a hand on the wall to steady herself.

"Are you all right," asked Joy.

Sally let out a cackling laugh. "I'm better than all right, dear. I'm the best."

The mahogany table in the formal dining room was laid out to seat seventeen: seven on one side, eight on the other, and Red and Kate at either end of the table. Everyone found the place card with a grape and wolf motif and their name and sat down. Max sat to Red's left, next to Sally, who sat beside her husband. Steele and Joy sat opposite Max. Lizzy, the guest of honor, sat beside Kate.

Max noted that Alice had not been given a seat at the table, and he knew it would not have been Kate's doing. Sally must have relegated her to kitchen duty.

Kate, Alice, and the maids swept into the room and offered each guest champagne for a toast, which everyone readily accepted, even Sally, despite the cringed faces of many who had hoped she'd politely decline.

Red raised his glass. "Lizzy, the day you came into our family, you blessed this house with love and kindness, and you blessed our hearts with joy. The good Lord needed Danny sooner than we expected, but we're here for you. We are your family, and we wish you a very 'appy birthday!"

Glasses rose in the air and chinked amidst additional wishes: "Here, here" or "Happy birthday, Lizzy."

Following the toast, Kate, Alice and the maids rushed back and forth between the kitchen and the dining room, setting a plate before guests, ladies first. Sally moved her plate and set it before Max. "I'm going to skip the salad." She rubbed her belly.

"You should eat," Max cajoled softly.

"I will, just not greenery on this stomach." Sally reached for her champagne and drank a large draught. She used her napkin to daub her face and forehead as if flushed.

Kate and the maids set down plate after plate, disappeared, and returned again until everyone had a salad, burgeoning with mixed greens, red and gold beets, goat cheese, and delicate white Queen Anne's Lace flowers.

Kate put her hands on Sally's shoulders. "I'll bring you a bowl of soup. Freshly made. It will set you right."

In no time, Kate returned and set a steaming bowl of potato and herb soup before Sally.

Kate took her seat, Red said grace, and forks clinked against the custom china, bearing the private logo of the estate—a wolf howling beside a bunch of grapes. Conversation erupted at each end of the table.

As the conversation drove forward into the night, Alice and the maids cleared the dishes. Kate helped serve the main course, which quickly disappeared amid praise for the chef, and in time, those empty plates disappeared too.

Kate excused herself to oversee dessert.

Maria dimmed the lights, and Kate rolled a cart into the room on which sat a sheet cake rimmed with colorful edible pansies. A cursive "Happy Birthday, Lizzy" message swirled across the center. A regiment of candles created light that danced over the white frosting.

Red insisted that everyone stand up for a song, which he began. Sally stayed seated, even though Elliot nudged her to stand. Everyone sang, "Happy birthday to you..."

Max felt odd. His hand trembled. He clenched and unclenched his fist and sang, "Happy birthday to you..."

Sally slurred. "Happy birthday, dear Daddy. Happy..."

Max eyed Sally, wondering if he'd heard her right—Daddy not Lizzy, but no one else seemed to pay her any attention, so he carried on until the final, "Happy birthday to you."

Max and the others sat back down. Max's vision blurred. He tried to blink it away. He stared at Joy, who pointed to her own chin, as if Max had something there.

Max reached up and felt drool. He wiped it away with his napkin. The room spun.

The maids cut the cake and set pieces on plates before the guests.

Max lifted his fork. His hand trembled.

Joy rose to her feet. "Max?"

Steele rose to his feet beside her.

Suddenly, Sally's arms convulsed. Muscle spasms twisted her neck and limbs. Her face contorted like a crazed monster having escaped an evil doctor's lab. Her head whipped back, and then slammed forward into her cake, where it remained.

Guests jumped up from the table. Cathy screamed.

Max's brows pinched with worry. His arms twitched. He shot a frightful look across the table. "What's happening?"

Joy raced around the table and pulled Sally's head out of the cake. She felt her neck for a pulse, while Red rushed to Max's side, along with Steele.

Sally looked as if she had slathered on a spa facial mask and now she napped. Joy felt for a pulse. "She's dead."

"Dead!" and "How?!" burst from the crowd. Cathy wailed. The others hung back to let Joy and Steele do their jobs.

Joy held the lids of Max's eyes open and saw fear. She tried not to show her own. "Dilated pupils!" She pressed her fingers against Max's wrist. "Rapid pulse." Joy barked commands. "Call for an ambulance. They've been poisoned!"

"Poison!" rose up from the crowd. Fearful, the guests watched for signs in one another or clamped on to their loved ones for fear of losing them.

Reed dialed his cell phone and stepped to a quieter place near the doorway.

Joy's eyes swept around the room. She inspected what was left of the cake. A bloom of edible pansies—purple, yellow, lavender and red—covered the edges of the cake. Joy inspected Sally's cake, which was hard to do, since it had been smashed.

Joy reached for a small cluster of tiny white flowers that stuck out from the frosting. She remembered seeing the same white flowers on the salads. Her eyes flew to a vase of flowers on the sideboard. Joy raced over to inspect it. Umbrella-shaped clusters of white flowers bloomed atop long, green stems with purple splotches. "The blood of Socrates," she whispered to herself.

"Ambulances and police are on the way," Steele shouted.

Joy pointed to the vase. "Hemlock. Help me move Max to the floor."

Steele grabbed Max under his arms, while Joy moved his chair. Steele laid Max on the oriental carpet.

Max's limbs jerked in spasms.

Joy leaned closer, and with her hand, she wiped away more drool from Max's chin.

Sirens wailed in the distance.

Red rushed out of the room to open the gates.

Joy shouted in a voice Max had never heard before. The calm monotone girl vanished, and a hysterical girl appeared in her place. "Stay with me, Max!" Joy shouted it so loudly, her voice rasped. "You hear me! Stay with me! You can't leave me!"

With her hand trembling from fear, Joy took Max's hand in hers. She interlocked her fingers in his, lay her head against his chest, and waited for the ambulance. All she could do was listen to Max's chest for signs of difficulty in breathing.

Joy would not let him go. Never again!

AUTHOR'S NOTE

Thank you for spending time with me in Wine Valley. While each novel can be read as a stand-alone murder mystery, Max and Joy's personal quest to discover their bizarre past will unravel more with each book, so you may want to read them in order.

The suspects' secret lives will continue to add unexpected twists, romances will build, all amidst harrowing danger and emotional upheavals. What more could one ask for than bizarre tales of murder and heart-stopping suspense in a pristine setting with old friends and new ones.

If you like the series, please leave a review and comment on Amazon. Word of mouth is incredibly powerful. A few words or a phrase or a sentence—it all helps. *And I'm grateful!*

Note: I use beta-readers, professional editors, and I proofread several times, but if you spot an error, please email me at sandra@sandrawoffington.com. Any errors are on me—not on my fabulous team.

PINOT NOIR AND POISON

WINE VALLEY MYSTERY BOOK 2

Pushed past a threshold, anyone can kill.

Det. Max King and Dr. Joy Burton enjoy a dinner party at a winery. A woman keels over at the table. Max does too.

In this heart-stopping suspense, suspects cross boundaries, reminding Joy of her own walks across fragile bridges that crumbled, leaving her stranded on a cold, desolate shore.

Cross over, and you can't always cross back.

Max and Joy continue their quest to unravel childhood secrets, hoping the truth will not become toxic to their lives.

You'll love this plunge into darkness! Return to Wine Valley. Pick up *Pinot Noir and Poison*.

BOOKS IN THE WINE VALLEY MYSTERY SERIES

Prequels:
Merlot and Murder: The Beginning (FREE)
Beaunoir and Blood: For Joy (FREE)
Grand Cru and Gangs: Steele's Story (Dead Silent Boxed Set)

The Series:
Burgundy and Bodies, Book 1 (May 2019)
Pinot Noir and Poison, Book 2 (May 2019)
Syrah and Swingers, Book 3 (May 2019)
Rose and Rocks, Book 4 (June 2019)
Grenache and Graves, Book 5 (Aug. 2019)
Shiraz and Slaughter, Book 6 (Sept. 2019)
Pinot Grigio and Pesticide, Book 7 (Nov. 2019)
Gamay Noir and Ghouls, Book 8 (Feb. 2020)
Claret and Carnage, Book 9 (May 2020)
Viognier and Venom, Book 10 (July 2020)
Frascati and Fratricide, Book 11
Fume Blanc and Fire, Book 12

Wine Valley Mystery Books 1-4 Boxed Set
Wine Valley Mystery Books 5-8 Boxed Set

More murder, mystery, and mayhem to come . . .

OTHER BOOKS BY THE AUTHOR

WARRIORS & WATCHERS SAGA SERIES

Epic Mythological Fantasy

Seven ancient gates of evil will open, unless a quirky group of teens become warriors.

"Original and consistently entertaining from cover to cover." **Midwest Book Review**

Evil Speaks (Reader's Favorite 5-Star Review)

Evil Hears (coming soon)

Evil Sees

Evil Touches

Evil Feeds

Evil Deeds

Evil Desires

———

STAND ALONE HISTORICAL ROMANCE

Unveiling

What would you sacrifice to fulfill your destiny?

STAY UP TO DATE

In appreciation of each and every reader, I created a Facebook group called *Woffington's Reading Warriors: Mystery, Murder, Magic & More* specifically for readers to join together and share their interests, discuss books, and to communicate directly with me and fellow Reading Warriors!

I post updates, previews, new releases, insider information, and awesome offers in this group.

Visit my website at sandrawoffington.com.

Follow me on Amazon, Facebook or Instagram.

Come for the Mystery—Stay for the Magic!

Printed in Great Britain
by Amazon

19784597R00128